Peter Conway lives in Somerset. He is a prolific writer and has also written *Unwillingly to School* and *Locked In*.

DESERVING DEATH

Sixteen-year-old Sophie Hammond's parents are desperately worried by her moods and withdrawn behaviour. Fearing that she might be taking drugs, they send Sophie as a boarder to Sandford College, a private school. When she's found dead in her room, it's assumed that she has either taken her own life, or accidentally overdosed on drugs. However Rawlings, the forensic pathologist, is convinced that she has been suffocated. Then there are two further deaths . . . The lives of all those involved, including the investigating police officers, are turned upside down before the answers to the tragedy are found.

Books by Peter Conway
Published by The House of Ulverscroft:

MURDER IN DUPLICATE
VICTIMS OF CIRCUMSTANCE
CRADLE SNATCH
ONE FOR THE ROAD
CRYPTIC CLUE
LOCKED IN
UNWILLINGLY TO SCHOOL

PETER CONWAY

◆

DESERVING DEATH

Complete and Unabridged

ULVERSCROFT
Leicester

First published in Great Britain in 2007 by
Robert Hale Limited
London

First Large Print Edition
published 2008
by arrangement with
Robert Hale Limited
London

The moral right of the author has been asserted

British Library CIP Data

Conway, Peter, *1929* –
　　Deserving death.—Large print ed.—
　　Ulverscroft large print series: crime
　　1. Boarding school students—Fiction
　　2. Detective and mystery stories 3. Large type books
　　I. Title
　　823.9′14 [F]

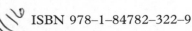 ISBN 978–1–84782–322–9

Published by
F. A. Thorpe (Publishing)
Anstey, Leicestershire

Set by Words & Graphics Ltd.
Anstey, Leicestershire
Printed and bound in Great Britain by
T. J. International Ltd., Padstow, Cornwall

This book is printed on acid-free paper

1

The figure, dressed all in black, cut the engine of the Ducati and coasted down the long incline, pulling up just short of the heavy iron gates set into the brick wall. This wall was some eight feet in height and stretched for several hundred yards in either direction. There was a small copse almost opposite the gates and the machine was run across a grass verge, along a narrow path and into a clearing. The bike, now hidden from the road, was turned so that it was facing the path and propped against a tree, the ground being too soft for its stand to be used.

The driver swapped the crash helmet for a balaclava, took off the boots and leathers to reveal a black, roll-necked, long-sleeved shirt and tight-fitting black trousers and put on similar coloured climbing shoes and thin gloves. Having stowed the discarded clothing in the twin panniers, the wide belt with a series of pouches set into it was strapped on and after listening intently at the edge of the copse for a minute or two, the figure moved swiftly and obliquely across the road to a point some fifty yards beyond the electrically operated gates. As expected, inspection of the top of the wall with the slim but powerful torch, revealed no evidence of barbed, razor nor electric wiring on the top and within seconds it was surmounted without any difficulty — there were even reasonable hand and footholds in the worn brickwork.

It was almost too easy — a few challenges to overcome always increased the satisfaction of a job well done. In this and all other forays meticulous preparation had been made. It had also been ascertained that the only dog on the property was a fat Labrador, which invariably slept next to the Aga in the kitchen; there were no burglar alarms and, being a listed building, there was no double glazing and the only man in the house was the elderly and stately butler.

A circuit of the outside of the building confirmed that the easiest windows to tackle on the ground floor were those of the dining-room, which was to the right of the front door. As there was a paved terrace in front of these, there would be no telltale footprints.

After applying suckers to the glass, a wide circle was cut out, carefully laid on the grass well clear of the house and the lock on the sash window opened at the second attempt with an instrument from the belt. There was no stop on the frame. After the window had been gently eased up a few inches, there was the faintest of squeaks. Immediately, grease was applied to the runnels on both sides, the window was very carefully moved down and up again, this time a little higher until there was further resistance; the procedure was repeated until there was a wide enough gap to permit entry into the room inside.

The door from the dining-room to the large hall was open. It was here that the stone staircase wound upwards on one side to a balcony and the figure waited in the hall for a good two minutes listening intently. The only sound was the loud tick from the grandfather clock and the bolts of the front door were then oiled and pulled back; the large key, still in the lock, was turned and the door eased open. Once again at the first hint of resistance, the hinges were oiled and when it moved freely and soundlessly it was left a few inches open.

Once the door to the drawing-room, which was on the opposite side of the hall to the dining-room, had been opened without incident, the narrow beam of the torch picked out the glass-fronted cabinet, which contained what the intruder was after. Satisfied that there were no obstructions in the way, the figure crept across the carpet and set to work on the lock. It proved trickier than expected and several minutes went by before, with a faint click, the metal tongue slipped across and the door of the cabinet swung open.

The torch was left on the bottom shelf, its beam directed towards the back of the cabinet and very gently the intruder began to feed one piece after another into the leather pouch. The operation was nearly over when the room was suddenly flooded with light and as the figure in black jerked upright and looked round, there was just time to see the shape behind and then the base of the heavy brass candlestick landed with a sickening thud on the top of the robber's head, who was thrown forwards against the cabinet and then slid sideways on to the floor.

The middle-aged woman stood over the prostrate figure, the candlestick still in her hand and bending forward slightly, failed to see the scything movement of the burglar's leg, which took her behind the knee. She fell awkwardly and was just beginning to get up when the large glass paperweight, which had been snatched up from a nearby table, hit the side of her head with sickening force.

The intruder stood for a moment, hand on head, swaying from side to side and then, pausing only to pick up the torch and the leather pouch, staggered towards the door, cannoning into a table, which fell sideways, the tall china vase on it shattering against the wooden wainscot. By the time the burglar had reached the hall, lights were already visible on the balcony above. Just having the presence of mind to lock the front door from the outside, the robber tottered in a travesty of a run towards the gate. Had it not been for a large tree stump under the wall not far from the gate, climbing over would not have been possible; as it was, once on top, the intruder half fell down to the ground on the other side, landing in a heap and moaning in agony.

If the motorcycle had been on its stand, pulling it off would have proved an impossibility. Also knowing that if it fell on its side there would have been no hope of righting it, the burglar used every last ounce of strength and concentration to get it vertical. Although expecting to hear a police siren at any moment and to see a flashing blue light, the intruder was forced to wait until the intense nausea and feeling of faintness had subsided. The self starter was then pressed, the headlight switched on and somehow the Ducati was navigated along the narrow path, turned onto the road and driven back up the hill.

2

'Your mother and I have decided to send you to Sandford College as a boarder next term.'

Sophie Hammond had long since discovered that silence was both the safest and most effective way of dealing with both her parents and she kept looking over her father's left shoulder at the picture on the wall behind him.

'We're both worried about you. You have no friends, if you're not trawling up and down the pool, you're doing God knows what alone in your room, or else going off somewhere on your bike. I suppose we should be grateful that at least you go to the riding school, but I gather that you never meet anyone there, either. If there's anything troubling you, be it drugs or if you're in some sort of mess, whatever it is, we're here to help you, surely you know that.'

Out of the corner of her eye, Sophie saw her mother shake her head in a gesture of defeat.

'When do I have to go?'

'Term starts in two weeks and your mother and I will take you up to London to fit you out with the uniform and the other things you'll need.' There was a long pause. 'Don't you want to hear about the school?'

Sophie shrugged her shoulders, knowing that that would annoy her father more than anything she would have been able to find to say. It did. She saw the muscles of his neck tighten, but she hadn't expected him to lose control — he never did that, whatever the provocation — and he didn't then, either.

'It'll be lovely, dear. Thanks to your father, a new pool was built at the college in the summer and I've heard that the house-mother who'll be looking after you, is also a really good swimmer and diver herself, so you'll be able to get some expert tuition.'

Her mother was trying hard, but it was a bit late for that, Sophie thought. Later, though, when she had slept on the idea, she realised that it had something to commend it from her point of view. At least she would be able to get right away from her problems and the reproachful looks of her mother. And so she did make an attempt to show some interest on the train up to London. Her father told her that Sandford College was his old school, was near a village in the Thames' Valley and that it had only recently accepted girls into the sixth form.

'You'll have a room of your own, you'll be

able to use your lap-top, printer and the internet on the project you'll be expected to do. They don't allow anyone to have mobile phones, but you can ring up your mother whenever you want to. It all sounds very relaxed and informal and we've both met Miss Rainsford, the house-mistress, who seems a very pleasant woman.'

Her father never showed his emotions, but even so she detected some relief in his voice as she listened to him attentively for once. She even asked a question about what sort of project it would be.

'Your form mistress will discuss that with you, but why not give it some thought yourself before you go?'

Why, Sophie wondered, were both her parents trying so hard when her father had ignored her completely for months and her mother had seemed embarrassed by her very presence in the house? Had they discovered something?

Sophie had made it a point of honour not to cry whatever the provocation, but she did so twice before she went to Sandford College, once when she went riding with Tim Harvey for the last time and a second time when she said goodbye to her cat, Sammy. Tim was just so nice. He had been patient with her when she was learning to do simple and later more complicated jumps and, even though they hardly ever spoke more than a word or two to one another when they were out riding together, he indicated with little smiles that he enjoyed her company. He also had sensed that she didn't like to be touched and, although he was always there when she mounted, she had complete confidence that he wouldn't get too near unless she really needed help.

She was only too well aware that if she tried to say thank you and goodbye back at the stables, she might break down and so she picked a moment when they were walking their horses along a path through a wood. Her determination to keep tight control of herself lasted only a matter of moments, after only a few words, she, who never cried and could hardly bear to be touched by anyone, burst into tears and found comfort in his arms. By the time they got back to the stables, though, she had managed to get a grip on herself and managed to apologise without breaking down again.

Her mother had given Sammy to her for her sixth birthday. She had adored him right from the beginning. Then, he had been a playful black kitten, now he was a sleek and affectionate ten-year-old; he seemed to sense when she was upset or close to utter despair and would jump up on to her lap, settle facing her and then look at her with his unblinking amber eyes, purring softly.

'Look after Sammy while I'm away, won't you, Mum, and don't forget Oscar, either. He's really important and I'd like to take him with me, but the other girls would think I was a baby if I took a teddy with me and would only laugh at me. Promise me you'll take very special care of him.'

'Of course I will, dear.'

Sophie could see how upset her mother was and had her father not been standing at the front door, making impatient clicking noises with his tongue, she would have given her a hug.

Most of her fears about Sandford College proved unfounded. Miss Rainsford, her house-mistress, was both friendly and not in the least threatening and her form mistress had long discussions with her about her project. She remembered what an effect the film, 'The Rabbit-Proof Fence', had had on her which she had seen on her lap-top when she had hired the CD from the public library in Esher. That film had given her the idea of writing about the white colonisation of Australia and the effects it had had on the aboriginal population and her teacher had been most enthusiastic about her plan.

Sophie had become almost obsessed with the task, spending most of her spare time using her lap-top and researching on the internet.

If she was getting on well with the staff, the same was not true of the other girls in her house. At least, though, they left her alone, except, that was, for the head of the house, Charlotte Winslow. Sophie hated to be seen with nothing on and squirmed with embarrassment when Charlotte had come barging into her room one evening when she was washing at the basin. The girl hadn't even apologised, brusquely telling her that there was a bolt on the door if she was that sensitive.

What Sophie enjoyed most, though, was the swimming. It wasn't only that the pool was really excellent, but Rob Preston, the college water-polo captain, joined her in the early morning and late afternoon training sessions and not only was he good competition, but she also liked him. Quite unlike Tim at the riding school, he was tall and powerfully built, but despite that was not in the least threatening. He always had a smile for her, never seemed to resent the fact that, despite his greater strength, he wasn't able to swim as fast as she could and he was a mine of information about swimming and swimmers, not least about Ian Thorpe, the

11

Australian, who was her special hero.

And then there was Jo Roberts, who supervised their early morning and late afternoon sessions. Sophie had never met anyone remotely like her before. Slim, but muscular, she was an absolutely brilliant performer on the spring board and trampoline and was no mean swimmer, either. She was no match for Sophie in the freestyle, they were roughly equal in the back stroke, but she was streets ahead of her in breast stroke and butterfly, in neither of which Sophie had ever trained seriously. That wasn't the half of it. Unlike the teachers at her other school, who had very much left her to her own devices, Jo took a great interest in the class-work she was doing and although at times brutally direct, wasn't in the least threatening or upsetting.

It had begun when she was practising her starts and was standing on the edge of the pool again after having done two of them.

'Don't move a muscle until I get back,' the woman said, turning and going through the swing doors into the gym, before coming back again almost immediately, pushing the full length mirror on its wheels.

'Now just look at yourself. You're like a wet sock, sagging in the middle. To win races, particularly sprints, you've got to have attitude and show some aggression. What are

12

you ashamed of? You've got great legs and a trim figure, so why not show a bit of pride. Pull your shoulders back and stand tall. That's better. Now, take your mark, get set, go!'

As Sophie pulled herself out of the water after two lengths flat out, Jo Roberts put her arm round her shoulders.

'That was great, much better, but why the flinching? I'm not going to eat you.'

Her warm smile took away any hint of threat and, after that, Sophie began to find the woman's enthusiasm infectious. It wasn't only in the pool. Miss Roberts showed her how to insert pictures into the text of her project, which she had scanned for Sophie on one of the scanners belonging to the college. She read through what Sophie had written, making constructive criticisms and, before she went to bed, Sophie would often share the freshly squeezed orange juice with her, which she bought at the college shop and liked to drink last thing at night.

It was on one such evening, after Sophie had been at the college for nearly six weeks, that Jo Roberts said to her:

'You're looking distinctly pasty, Sophie; you need some exercise out of doors and I'm going to take you riding next Sunday. I used to work for Mrs Farr, whose husband is on the Board of this place; they've got a country house not far from here and when I was there I used to exercise the neighbours' horses. We're invited to lunch and Miss Rainsford's checked that your father has no objection.'

'He won't be there, will he?'

'Worried about having to be on your best behaviour at lunch, are you? No, he won't and George Farr's not a bad sort, so you don't have to get worked up about him, either.'

Sophie felt as she imagined the people she had seen on TV white-water rafting must have done, carried along by an irresistible force, which in this instance was Jo's personality. With a free choice she would have refused the invitation, but she wasn't given one.

'I haven't got any kit.'

'Who needs kit? I'm just going to take a pair of jeans, a sweater and a change of underwear and the Calloways have a selection of hard hats, one of which is bound to fit you.'

In fact, the day was quite amazing for her. There was the drive there in Jo's Mazda which in itself was quite something. It was practically new, had vivid acceleration and, unlike the stately progress of her father's Mercedes, or her mother's anxious caution in her small Peugeot, Jo flung the car into the corners in controlled slides and when they arrived did a hundred and eighty degree handbrake turn in front of the house, sending up a shower of gravel.

Sophie managed to get through the lunch by virtue of saying almost nothing, except in response to Mr Farr's ponderous attempts to ask her about the college and keeping her eyes down while the man's wife, who was obviously in a foul mood, contradicted almost everything her husband said, while shooting malignant glances in her and Jo's direction. As for Jo, she didn't seem to be in the least put out, chatting to the young Scottish girl who was serving the lunch and then engaging George Farr in a long discussion about the difficulties of managing large estates and the expense of even basic maintenance of the buildings.

Afterwards, though, the riding proved to be one of the most exciting experiences of her life. The horses were hunters and for the first time she experienced the thrill of a long gallop and she jumped a natural fence. These were very different from the modest, manicured ones at the riding school that Tim had led her over.

When they got back, there was no sign of the Farrs and Jo took her into the ballroom, which had been converted into a gym.

'You go first,' she said, pointing towards the large shower cubicle in one corner. 'It's the only bit of plumbing that works properly in this dreary mausoleum and it's got its own electric water heater. I'll go and see if I can prise a couple of towels out of that grizzly woman who masquerades as a housekeeper.'

Sophie had expected Jo to pass her the towel around the side of the door, so that she could dry herself inside the cubicle and come out with it wrapped around her and was quite unprepared for the door being pulled open as soon as she turned the water off.

'Out you come.'

She tried desperately to cover herself up, but Jo, with her own towel tied just above her breasts, took her by the hand and almost pulled her out. She blushed crimson as the other woman draped the second towel over her shoulders then, facing her, dropped her own on to the floor.

'A body's just a body, you know, and yours is a great deal better than mine.' She patted her flat stomach and then ran her hands down the fronts of her thighs. 'I'm too muscular by half. The woman who ran the fitness centre where I used to work said I looked like a Russian weight lifter. Right, I won't be long.'

Jo also came to see her in her room that evening.

'I'm not going to apologise for the shock tactics this afternoon,' she said, 'but as I said the other day, if you are going to be any real good as a swimmer — and you have the potential to get to the very top — you've got to develop a presence. Did you see Ian Thorpe embarrassed and bending double to hide himself when he was waiting to get on to the blocks? No, you did not. He stood tall and confident, he wasn't in doubt, he dominated the others before they'd hit the water and it was all done without ostentation or gamesmanship. It's important for you to understand what I'm talking about. Do you?'

'Yes, I do, but . . . '

'No buts. Had a nice time today, did you?'

'Lovely, thank you, really great.'

'I'm so glad. Now, hop into bed and I'll see you at the pool tomorrow morning. Don't be late.'

The woman bent over her and having given her a quick kiss on the forehead, strode across the room. She smiled at Sophie from the door, waved and closed it carefully behind herself.

Sophie's radio alarm clock woke her at 6.30 the following morning, she was so stiff that it was only with the greatest difficulty that she was able to get out of bed and the sensation had hardly eased at all by the time she got to the pool. For once, she was unable to keep up with Rob Preston and when Jo took him into the gym to work with the weights, she turned on to her back and floated, trying to relax.

'What's up?'

'Stiff.'

'What you need is a hot shower and a massage. Out you get.' She handed the girl a towel and a robe as she climbed up the steps with considerable difficulty. 'Poor old you, you are in a bad way. Take the shower as hot as you can bear and then come into my office. I'll take your clothes for you.'

By the time Sophie had finished Rob Preston had already gone and she found Jo working on her computer. After knocking, Sophie opened the door in response to the loud 'come in'.

'Drink the stuff in that glass first — it's one of those solutions that marathon runners take and should ward off any cramp — then slip your robe off and lie face down on the couch under the sheet you'll find there,' she said without looking round. 'I'll be with you in a moment.'

Sophie did what she had been told, although initially terrified of what was going to happen, but gradually she relaxed as first the powder was sprinkled over her shoulders and then the strong fingers gradually began to ease the tension in her stiff and painful muscles. She opened her mouth to protest when the sheet was pulled up from below, but almost at once the warm hands began to knead her calves and she let out her breath in a long sigh. Very slowly the hands moved upwards and the most delicious sensation began to flood through the very centre of her and she almost wept with frustration when the sheet was pulled down again.

'I think that should do the trick. You don't want to be late for breakfast, do you?'

Sophie heard the click of the door closing, lay there for a moment without moving, her heart thumping painfully and then she slowly got up and dressed.

The following weekend they went riding again and this time the gallop was longer and the jumps more demanding and she felt utterly drained when it was over and she was sitting on the bench in the Farr's gym.

'I don't know about you,' Jo said, 'but I'm sweating like a pig and I don't fancy hanging around waiting for my shower — it's as cold as charity in here. Why don't we get in together? There's plenty of room for two and I need someone to soap my back — my right

19

shoulder's giving me a bit of grief.'

Sophie was embarrassed and scared, but at the same time excited by the suggestion. She was already feeling uncomfortably cold.

'Don't be too long.'

Jo gave her a grin as she began to slip out of her clothes and without conscious thought Sophie smiled back and her hands went to the bottom of her sweater. Had Jo taken the initiative when she stepped into the shower, Sophie would probably have taken fright, but she didn't, handing the girl the bar of soap and turning her back on her. Sophie was later to think that her hands almost had a life of their own as they soaped the skin of the firmly muscled shoulders and back, which felt so smooth and when, without thinking, she moved first to the armpits and then round to the front, feeling the rounded breasts and the hardening of the nipples, the shock went right through her.

'Thanks,' Jo said, turning her head, 'that was great, but I think I'd better take care of the rest, don't you?'

She did so quickly and efficiently, gave Sophie a grin and the thumbs up sign and then stepped out of the cubicle. Sophie was dreading having to face the woman when she had finished, but to her relief the gym was empty when she got out of the shower and on her return, Jo gave her a broad smile.

'Sorry to have kept you, but I had a bit of an altercation with the lady of the manor, but not to worry, that did nothing to spoil the fun I've had today — I hope it was the same for you.'

'Oh, it was. I can't thank you enough.'

In bed that evening, Sophie went over in her mind all that had happened since her parents had sent her to the college. To start with, she had been terrified, but it had turned out nothing like as bad as she had expected. True, she still hadn't made friends with any of the girls, but the more she saw of Rob Preston, the more she liked him. He was always so nice to her and never seemed to resent her greater skill in the pool nor that Jo Roberts constantly criticised his technique and gave him such a hard time. Her school work and project were also going well, Miss Rainsford continued to take an interest in what she was doing and as for Jo . . . she was fun, she spoke her mind and there was a lot more, which she preferred not to think about too deeply.

'Where's Rob?' she asked a few days later when he failed to turn up for the afternoon session.

'Oh, I forgot to tell you,' Jo replied, 'he can't make it today. I'm not sure why, but it'll give us a chance to put in some work on your turns.'

Jo really put her through it and afterwards there was a hot drink and the massage, which had become a regular occurrence, to look forward to. By now, Sophie had lost all her fears about undressing in front of Jo and on this occasion was feeling most peculiar; so relaxed that it almost seemed as if she was boneless, but at the same time the most extraordinary sensation was beginning to creep right through to the very centre of her. She didn't protest when, for the first time, the sheet was pulled down and right off. After working on her shoulders and back, Jo's strong fingers began to knead her calves, using an aromatic oil she moved up to her thighs and then to the firm muscles of her bottom. She let out a gasp as her legs were parted and when a finger slipped between them and began to slide up and down, her head came back and round, her eyes widened and her mouth opened.

'Don't stop,' she begged, 'please don't stop.'

Before she was fully able to appreciate what was going to happen, she was turned on to her back, pulled down to the end of the couch and her legs divided over Jo's shoulders. The woman stared down at her for a moment or two, her eyes wide open, then she lowered her head.

Later, snuggling up to Jo on the sofa in the house-mother's room, Sophie felt a sense of peace that she had never experienced before. It was then that she told Jo all about it. She hadn't even considered doing that to anyone before, let alone planned it, it just came out. Jo listened attentively to all she had to say without interrupting and when she had finished, gave her a hug.

'Poor you, I'm so sorry. What a terrible worry for you!'

'You won't tell anyone about this, will you?'

'No, of course not. I do need to let it sink in, though, and have a long think about how I might be able to help you. I'm so glad you told me, though, the worst thing you could have done would have been to kept it to yourself any longer. A trouble shared is a trouble halved, as my grandmother used to say.'

That night, though, as she lay in bed, unable to get off to sleep, doubts began to enter Sophie's mind. Apart from the worry that Jo might let it slip out, she didn't see how the woman would be able to help her. It wasn't only that; Sophie hadn't been able to come to terms with what had happened during that massage.

In the next few days, the routine of sessions in the pool continued and although Jo did not treat her in any way differently, was it her imagination or had Rob Preston's attitude towards her changed? It wasn't that he ignored her completely, but he hardly said anything and wouldn't look her in the eye, the easy companionship that they had shared seeming to have disappeared completely.

Miss Rainsford also noticed that something was wrong. 'Is anything worrying you, dear?' she asked. 'You don't look yourself at all.'

Sophie took refuge in the usual ready-made excuse of adolescent girls when they wanted to get out of something.

'Would you like to see the doctor? No? Well, why not have an early night and I'll ask Jo to bring you up a nice hot water bottle. You've got some panadol, have you?'

Jo did come that evening and explained that riding wouldn't be possible at the coming weekend.

'Mr Farr rang me up this afternoon to say that his wife wasn't well. He's not very good at covering up and, if you ask me, they've had one of their rows about something or other. Not to worry, though, this isn't the first time it's happened — they were always having dust-ups when I was working there — and I'm sure it will blow over quite quickly.

Anyway, it will give me the opportunity to have a chat to a solicitor about your problem. I got to know him well when I was working at a stunt school and I'm sure he'll give some good advice.'

Sophie felt as if a lump of ice had been dropped down inside the back of her pyjama jacket.

'Please don't do that.'

'I wouldn't mention your name or anything.'

'I'm sure you wouldn't, but he must know that you're working here and . . . '

'Very well, but you can't just do nothing, now can you?' Sophie shook her head miserably and looked away. 'Cheer up. Why not have a serious think about it over the weekend?'

Sophie did think about it, indeed she thought about nothing else while Jo was away and even though the woman spent a long time with her on the following Monday evening, she wasn't able to get the idea out of her mind that there was only one certain way of putting an end to her troubles for good, one that she had considered often enough. Perhaps after all, that would be the best solution and the time had come.

3

Jo Roberts strode along the corridor, stopped in front of the door of the room at the end of the corridor on the first floor of the building and knocked sharply on it.

'Quarter to eight, Sophie.'

When there was no response, she knocked again, this time more firmly and then, after waiting for a few moments and listening, turned the door knob and pushed. She felt it give a fraction, but then there was firm resistance.

'Sophie!' she called out even louder, listened once more, then turned and hurried down to the dining-room where Miss Rainsford was checking the cereal packets laid out on the sideboard.

'What's the problem, Jo?'

'It's Sophie, Miss Rainsford, her bedroom door's bolted and she's not answering even though I knocked and called out loudly.'

The house-mistress made a gesture with her hand towards the door and the two women hurried up the stairs and along the corridor. It was not in Margaret Rainsford's nature to hesitate and after calling out once and rattling the handle, she strode to the end of the corridor, lifted the fire extinguisher from its bracket and hit the door a powerful blow with its base. The door gave a fraction and then with the second attempt, it flew open. She took one brief look inside the room and then turned, all the colour drained from her face.

'You stay here and keep the other girls away, would you please, Jo?'

She went into the room, pulling the door to behind her and at that moment Jo heard footsteps from along the corridor and turned round sharply.

'It's all right, Claire, just go down to breakfast, would you? You're already late.'

The girl hesitated briefly, looking towards the damaged door, then turned and went down the stairs. Jo Roberts began to pace up and down until some two to three minutes later, Margaret Rainsford reappeared, whey-faced and with beads of sweat on her forehead.

'Is she all right?'

'No, she's not all right at all, Jo, she's dead.'

'Dead?'

'Yes. Now, I'm going down to my study to telephone Mr Manners and I want you to stand guard here until I get back. Is that clear?'

'Yes, Miss Rainsford.'

★ ★ ★

'I suppose you'll be wanting Sinclair again.'

Detective Superintendent Bill Watson's eyes narrowed slightly. 'You a mind reader or something, Alan? I know you don't like him, but can you suggest anyone better under these particular circumstances? You can't deny that he made a first-rate job of the Linda Baines case and he and DC Campbell work very well together.'

'Too well, if you ask me.'

Watson's expression suddenly changed and he stared at his deputy until the man's eyes dropped.

'I didn't ask you, Alan, and if those two continue to do their job to my satisfaction, what happens in their private life is no concern of mine, nor should it be of yours. Talk about old women gossiping! I'm looking to you to stamp that sort of thing out, not to propagate it; apart from anything else it's bad for morale, particularly if the senior staff indulge in it. I don't think I need say anything more on the subject, do I?'

'No, sir.'

'Good. Now, ask him to come up here right away, would you?'

Burgess was becoming a liability, Watson thought. No, he wasn't becoming one, he was one and something was going to have to be done about it and soon. He shook his head irritably, opened the file on his desk and was still studying it when he heard the soft knock on the door.

'Ah, Sinclair, good of you to have come up, have a seat.'

Ever since the man had arrived, Watson had felt distinctly uncomfortable in the presence of the tall, immaculately turned-out man on the other side of the desk. It wasn't just his public school and university background, but he seemed so detached from the other men and women in the Force that he had even thought there might be something behind the rumours that he was gay. Now, there was talk about him having an affair with the young Scottish DC, Fiona Campbell. Rumours, rumours, he was fed up with the bloody things. The fact was that Sinclair was far and away the best man for a tricky case like this.

'Know anything about Sandford College?'

'Not a great deal, sir. It's a public school, one of the many founded in the middle of the nineteenth century, I believe, and it's a few miles from Wantage. It takes girls in the sixth forms and I've heard that it has a good academic record, being somewhere in the middle of the second division of the league tables.'

Watson would have raised his eyebrows had he been less adept at hiding his emotions — he had never heard of the place himself until the present business had cropped up.

'Girl by the name of Sophie Hammond was found dead in her room one morning in one of the female boarding houses at the end of last week. At first it looked as if she might have taken an overdose of sleeping tablets or died from a reaction to one of those fancy pep pills that are so fashionable with the young these days, but for some reason Rawlings has his doubts, although he's not prepared to give his reasons just yet — you know what the man's like — and he wants to carry out some more tests. There's nothing like uncertainty to make situations like this more difficult, not to mention that both her father and Hastings, the Chief Constable, are on the board of the college. Everything's bound to come out at the inquest, but before that, considerable tact will be required until we get a definite answer from Rawlings. The body has of course already been removed, but I've arranged for one of the scene-of-crime men to show you the room at eleven, which will give you the opportunity to make your number with the headmaster beforehand — I've already warned him that you'll be coming. You'll find the details, such as they are, in this folder. By the way, you'd better take DC Campbell with you. She proved very useful in the Linda Baines case, as I recall, and I don't need to tell you that making enquiries about adolescent girls can prove a tricky proposition.'

'What about the girl's parents?'

'I've already spoken to the father, Derek Hammond, on the phone and all I said was that the girl had been found dead and that an overdose was suspected. He'd like to see you as soon as possible and I suggest that you ring his secretary for an appointment directly after you've had a chance to look round the college and talked to the house-mistress who found the girl. You'll find a copy of his entry in 'Who's Who' in the folder.'

★ ★ ★

'Would you drive and I'll tell you as much as I've been able to discover from all this bumf?'

Before starting the engine, Fiona Campbell glanced across at the man beside her, who was sorting out the papers on his lap. What had gone wrong? At the end of the Linda Baines case, everything had seemed to be going so well between them and yet by the time she had recovered from the shock and physical effects of the injuries she had received, all the old formality had returned. Was it that she had misjudged the situation and that he had merely been reacting with concern to what had happened to her? God, she thought, angry with herself, I'm behaving like a character in a Mills & Boon novel.

'Right,' Sinclair said a few minutes later. 'This girl, Sophie Hammond was the daughter of a prominent businessman who also happens to be a Governor of the college and an acquaintance of Hastings, the Chief Constable, who also sits on the Board. She had only been there since the start of the autumn term, six weeks ago. She was sixteen, seemingly having settled in fairly well, albeit rather lacking in friends, when last Tuesday, she failed to come down to breakfast and the housemother, as they call the woman who looks after the girls' general welfare, went up to her room and found the door bolted on the inside — none of them is fitted with a key. She fetched the house-mistress, who broke the door open and found the girl dead. The headmaster was contacted and the school doctor sent for. The doctor was sufficiently uneasy about the situation not to want to disturb the body apart from satisfying himself that she really was dead and insisted that everyone was kept away until the police arrived.'

'Has he given his reasons?'

'There's nothing in here about that and we'll obviously have to have a word with him on that score. Rawlings is also keeping his cards very close to his chest; he has already done the autopsy, but is evidently waiting for the results of some tests before committing himself to a cause of death.'

'What's our plan this morning?'

'We've clearly got to make our number with the headmaster first and then we're due to meet the scene-of-crime man at eleven. Let's hope that the former is not too touchy — I can't think of anything much worse for him to have to cope with.'

Guy Manners was a powerfully-built man in his middle fifties, his massive shoulders betraying the fact that he had been a stalwart of the Harlequins rugby team for many years and a trialist for England. His manner was as direct as his play in the scrum had been.

'I must confess,' he said, 'that my immediate reaction when your Chief Constable rang to tell me that it was in the interests of both the parents and the college that this matter should be looked into carefully, was to think that we might be stirring up a hornets' nest all for nothing. I know just enough about the subject to realise that young people can die suddenly for purely medical reasons and if that was the case, why all the fuss? A few moments' reflection, though, was enough for me to understand what would happen if I was seen to be trying to hush things up if, say, the girl had taken an overdose, either deliberately, or by accident. Of course I understand why your people can't be too careful, press interest in this sort of thing being what it is.'

'How many people here know about a possible overdose?'

'Well, as far as the college is concerned, only Miss Rainsford, the girl's house-mistress, who found the girl dead in bed, Dr McIntosh and I. I trust both of them implicitly and they gave me an undertaking that they wouldn't discuss the business with anyone else apart from the police, but I'm sure I don't need to tell you how easily rumours can spread in a place like this.'

'What about the girl's parents? I gather that her father is a member of the Board.'

'That's right. I know Derek Hammond reasonably well and rang him up straight away. As well as being on the Board, he's an old boy of the college. He's been extremely generous to us and recently financed the refurbishment of our large Victorian gymnasium, so that now it's a fitness centre and the swimming pool adjacent to it has been enlarged and proper changing rooms and showers are now available for both facilities. That cost a tidy sum, I can tell you.'

'What exactly did you tell him when you rang?'

'Just the bald facts that Sophie had been found dead in bed and that a possible drug overdose was suspected.'

'How did he react to that?'

'Hammond is not the sort of person who tolerates people beating about the bush in their dealings with him, as I know well from direct experience, and, as I expected, he was very controlled, but what I had not anticipated was his immediate offer of the services of one of his personal assistants who handles his press relations.'

'And did you take up the suggestion?'

'Indeed I did and the man has proved invaluable already. I must confess that my immediate thought was that Hammond's reaction was both detached and unemotional, but then he's that sort of man. On reflection I realised that those heart-rending and tearful interviews of parents on TV, which I happen to think help nobody, would never have been his way and unwise comments from someone like me, who has no experience of that sort of pressure, might lead to all sorts of extra problems.'

'What about the girl's mother?'

'Hammond said he'd break the news to her himself.'

'Have you said anything to the other pupils?'

'Yes, I called a special assembly before the rumours could start spreading and that is where Hammond's man came in very useful. He advised me to say as little as possible, just that Sophie had been found dead in her room early that morning and that the police and doctors were in the process of trying to find out what exactly had happened. I thought it wise to ask Hammond's man whether I should warn the pupils about the press, luckily he agreed to do that himself and he put it all a great deal better than I would have done.'

'Has the presence of girls here led to a lot of extra difficulties?'

'It certainly has and not only logistical ones. I won't pretend that I was happy when the Board took the decision to admit them to the sixth form here, but I went along with it; in fact, we didn't have much choice, our numbers were going down and we had to follow the trend. It's not that I was entirely opposed to the idea in principle, but this place was not designed for girls and we had to make a great many changes. There have been some pluses, but there has been a downside as well. The boys are not performing in class as well as they used to and there has been a dramatic drop in the standard of games. There are those on the Board who think that that is no bad thing, but I am not one of them. In my day at a school such as this, there was continuous activity and sex and drugs were no problem. The talk about places of this kind being hotbeds of homosexuality in the past is grossly exaggerated.'

'Have you had difficulties with sex and drugs here, then, recently?'

'Not so far, apart from some cannabis smoking, which created something of a furore last year. I had already instituted a zero tolerance policy, which was made crystal clear to all parents and children and we expelled the two offenders, a boy and a girl. One set of parents did make a fuss, but the Board, with one or two tiresome exceptions, were behind me and we weathered it without too much publicity. As to sex; well, all I can say is that nothing's surfaced so far. There have been no pregnancies and no one has been caught in flagrante, but it would be naïve to believe that a few haven't managed to find a way. Perhaps the fairest way of putting it would be to say that parents and, for that matter, agony aunts and the so-called experts are no better at dealing with adolescent problems in that direction than we are. We arranged for the female partner of our long-standing school doctor to take on formal sex instruction and advice for the girls and McIntosh continues to do that for the boys.'

'Did you know Sophie Hammond at all yourself?'

'Not directly, no. I make a point of seeing all the new girls and boys in a group on their arrival and saying a few words of welcome. The rest I leave to the house-masters and mistresses. It is not a good idea for a headmaster to interfere with their responsibilities. I worked at a school similar to this once, as a house-master and I remember how I resented the head poking his nose into what I considered was my province. I think it might be a good idea for you to have a word with Miss Rainsford; she's taking a class at the moment, but that'll be over in about ten minutes and after that she'll be in her study in her house. I did warn her that you might be coming, but if it's not convenient, we can easily find another time.'

Sinclair glanced at his watch. 'No, that would suit us well. We've already taken up enough of your time,' he said, smiling, 'why don't DC Campbell and I take a turn around the grounds before seeing her? Oh, one last thing, may I have the school doctor's phone number? I'd like to have a word with him.'

'Of course. Janet will be able to give it to you on your way out and she'll also point out the way to Miss Rainsford's house. By the way, you'd better have the number of my mobile as well; I can't stand the bloody things, but they do have their uses.'

When he had thanked the man, Sinclair walked slowly round the perimeter of the games' field with Fiona in the direction of the girls' boarding houses.

'What did you make of him?' he asked.

'I was rather impressed — he seems very direct and straight forward. I was half expecting a catalogue of reasons why we shouldn't disrupt the school's activities by taking staff away from their duties, complaints that we would stir up trouble with parents if we interviewed any of the boys and girls, that we were making too much of a fuss about it and so on. In the event, he couldn't have been more helpful.'

Sinclair smiled. 'You mustn't get too cynical, you know. There are still plenty of reliable and honest people about. On the other hand one mustn't be too swayed by first impressions and we certainly mustn't jump to firm conclusions on the evidence of one brief meeting.'

★ ★ ★

'*La police*, Henry, *la*! How many more times do I have to tell you that although the French keep boasting about the logicality of their language, there are exceptions and this is one of them, although less illogical than it used to be with so many women taking up police work now as a career. It's a mistake I might just understand if you hadn't made it before and the fact that you're reading makes it worse — concentrate for goodness' sake.'

It was so unlike Miss Rainsford to snap at her class that the atmosphere changed abruptly, the tension becoming almost palpable. They were already upset, of course they bloody well were, she said to herself, and what on earth was she doing adding to their distress?

'Look,' she said, 'I'm sorry, I'm not myself today.'

It had been the word 'Police' that had sparked it off, that and the knowledge that in all probability she would be seeing the Inspector after the class. The tragedy of one of her girls seemingly having taken her own life was bad enough, but why were the police involved and why did they want to see her?

She had been expecting a thick-set, bullet-headed bully bursting out of a blue serge suit so she was quite unprepared for the tall, pleasant-looking man, who smiled as he introduced himself and his assistant in a cultivated voice. The other surprise was the young woman with him. It wasn't that she looked anything like Sophie, but it was her facial expression and body language, waif-like and with a slightly hang-dog appearance that reminded her so strongly of the girl.

'This must be a very difficult time for you,' the man said.

'It is and worst of all is the feeling that I ought to have realised just how depressed and desperate the girl must have been.'

The detective nodded. 'First of all, would you tell me exactly how you found her.'

'She was lying with the bedclothes almost covering her completely. I called out to her and when there was no response drew the sheet and blankets down a little. She was lying almost completely on her front with her head turned to the left. I could just see that her left eye was open and that she wasn't breathing. I thought later that at least I ought to have tried artificial respiration, but don't ask me how, I just knew she was dead and, to be honest I couldn't bear the thought of having to touch her.'

'I can understand that.' Sinclair said. 'What did you do next?'

'Miss Roberts, who had alerted me to the fact that Sophie hadn't answered her call and that the door was bolted, stayed to guard the door to prevent any of the girls from going in. I went to fetch Mr Manners.'

The detective nodded. 'Tell me about Sophie.'

'She was in a group of new girls who started at the beginning of this term. She seemed much younger for her age than the others, less self assured and obviously not good at making friends. That's why I asked Charlotte, the house captain, to look after her. The fact that that didn't prove to be a success was more my fault than either of theirs. Charlotte is one of those girls who was born a head prefect and although she is far too mature to gossip to me about any of the girls, I should have realised that she wouldn't be exactly motherly with Sophie. She's all for effort and doing one's best and, as you may imagine she goes down extremely well with the headmaster and indeed with the captains of the boys' houses, but she's hardly the right person for the shy and introverted girl who Sophie seemed to be. It's not fair to run Charlotte down, though, although a bit on the 'jolly hockey sticks' side of the average, she's a good-hearted and thoroughly capable young woman.'

'Did Sophie have any obvious worries apart from settling into a new and very different school from her previous one?'

'There was nothing specific that I knew of, she just seemed, if not exactly depressed, flat and very much kept herself to herself. Indeed, that's why her father sent her here; he was worried about that himself, telling me that she had no friends and when not at school, used to spend hours swimming up and down in the pool that the Hammonds have in their house and going for long solitary walks or rides at one of the local equestrian schools.'

'Did you have any suspicion that she might have had sleeping pills or any other drugs in her possession?'

'None at all. We have a strict rule here that all medication, with one or two exceptions, such as small amounts of paracetamol, antihistamines for those with hay fever, inhalers for asthma and some topical skin preparations, has to be checked and given out by the house-mother.'

'How did she get on with her school work?'

'That was something I did worry about a bit. You see, she was undoubtedly a bright girl, if not a really high flier, but she suffered from being over conscientious and used to spend hours on her lap-top working on her project.'

'What was it on?'

'The early white settlement of Australia and the privations they experienced on their way there and during the early days. To be honest, I'm not a great fan of course work. It bores the pants off the really clever and favours the obsessional and conscientious, like Sophie. They tend to copy reams of stuff from the Internet, but at least Sophie was doing some reading as well.'

'How about games?'

'She wasn't interested in the organised variety, but she had a real talent as a swimmer — Miss Roberts told me that with proper coaching she could have been of international standard. I thought she needed encouragement and support in that direction so she was allowed to get her exercise in that way. Another bonus was that according to Jo, she seemed to get on well with one of the boys, the college's water polo captain, who is also having extra swimming tuition.'

'Miss Roberts?'

'I'm sorry, I ought to have explained. Jo is the house-mother. She's only been here since the start of last summer term and although it was immediately obvious that she was going to be a great asset to the college as a swimming instructor and in the gym, I must confess that I had doubts about her abilities in the house — on the face of it, she's not exactly, a motherly person. I asked her once why she didn't apply for a post as a games' mistress somewhere and she said that as she didn't have a degree, she wouldn't have a chance and, in any case, she was quite happy with what she was doing. In fact, she has proved to be extremely good with things such as the supervision of the laundry and health matters and quite the opposite of Mrs Frampton, her predecessor, who was an absolute dear and much loved by the girls, but efficient she most certainly was not.'

'Did Mrs Frampton retire?'

'No, she had a fall on an escalator last Easter on the underground in London and broke her hip.'

'Is she going to come back?'

'She was certainly expected to, but to be thoroughly indiscreet, I wasn't disappointed when she decided against it — she was already a bit past it.'

'How did Sophie get on with Miss Roberts?'

'I must say that I misjudged Jo in that respect; she proved to be absolutely brilliant with Sophie.'

'In what way?'

'One of the mistakes that it is easy to make when dealing with girls who are shy, passive and young for their age is to treat them as if they are babies incapable of fitting in — I even found myself putting on my 'children's hour' voice when talking to her, for God's sake. Jo never did that; she spoke to her very directly in exactly the same way as she did to everyone else, wasn't afraid to tell her to pull her socks up if she was moping and not trying as hard as she might in the swimming pool. She also took an interest in her project and spent quite a bit of time helping her with it in her room. Sophie was having problems with her lap-top and Jo is also good at that sort of thing, which is more than could be said of me. I never have been able to get the hang of the beastly things.'

'Did Miss Roberts' efforts work?'

'They were beginning to. Sophie seemed to have a pathological dislike of being touched and yet one day recently when she was obviously upset about something, I saw Jo put her arm round her shoulders and she didn't flinch or pull away, which I had seen happen when one of the other girls tried the same thing. Before she came here, Jo used to work for Mr Farr, another board member, who has a large house only a few miles from here; both he and Mr Hammond are old boys of the college, and she took Sophie there for Sunday lunch and to have a ride on a couple of occasions. I did check with Mr Hammond before allowing her to go and he said that it was he himself who had made the suggestion as riding was one of Sophie's only interests apart from swimming — he even apologised for not having asked for my agreement before the invitation was sent.'

'How did Sophie view that idea?'

'After some initial hesitation, for once she became really enthusiastic. She obviously liked Jo and a bonus was that she is also an excellent rider. Jo's into all of that sort of thing: gymnastics, diving, bungee jumping and driving fast cars, you name it, she's done it. Once, I gather, she worked as an instructor at a school for stunt men and women in films and that's not something that any other member of staff here has on their CV, I can tell you.'

Sinclair smiled. 'That I can well believe. I imagine that both you and Miss Roberts must have been deeply upset by Sophie's death.'

'I was completely shattered, but as Mr Manners said to me, life has to go on and there are the other girls under my care to think about, too. As for Jo, she is a much less emotional and more controlled person than me and she provided the support I needed. She pointed out that for either of us to go round with long faces the whole time wasn't going to help anyone and I think she was right. I'm not suggesting for one moment that she wasn't deeply affected — after all, she had seen more of Sophie than any other member of staff — she was just able to handle it better than some of us and that includes me.'

'Did Sophie ring home very often? I gather that mobiles aren't allowed, but presumably there are payphones available, or something similar.'

'Yes, there are, but I don't know. I have to strike a balance between keeping a careful eye on all of them and yet not intruding.'

'What about alcohol?'

'If twelve-year-olds at Cheltenham Ladies' College can be found drunk and incapable, then it can happen anywhere, but it's never been a problem in this house. As far as Sophie was concerned, I couldn't see her breaking any rule, let alone drinking. She used to like to have freshly squeezed orange juice last thing at night, which she used to buy at the college's tuck shop. She offered me some once when I was saying goodnight to her and as it was the first spontaneous gesture she had made to me, I accepted.'

'Did Sophie show any sign of being particularly depressed, or upset recently?'

'Well, I did notice that she was looking

rather down at the end of the week before she died and I even asked her about it. She told me that it was just the time of the month; as you may imagine that's a pretty common problem in a place like this and what I did was suggest that she perhaps should take a panadol and I asked Jo to take her a hot water bottle that evening and keep a special eye on her.'

'After you'd come out of Sophie's room on the morning when you broke into it, would anyone else have had the opportunity to go in there before our men arrived?'

'Mr Manners did take a look in there with me and also the school doctor, but apart from us, no one. I had already asked Jo to stand guard outside the door in the corridor and, at the head's suggestion, she remained there until your people came on the scene.'

Sinclair nodded. 'I'd like to have a word with Miss Roberts after we've had a look at Sophie's room, what would be the best way to get hold of her?'

'I'll be here for the rest of the morning and I'll page her for you when you're ready.'

Sinclair smiled. 'Thank you, you've been most helpful. Have you any questions for Miss Rainsford, Fiona?'

'Not for the moment, thank you.'

49

The house-mistress showed them both to the door and stood for a moment watching them as they started along the corridor. The tall detective, she thought, was a most attractive man.

4

'Good morning, sir.'

Bert Harris, the scene-of-crime man was waiting for them in the corridor outside Sophie Hammond's room. Sinclair acknowledged his greeting with a smile.

'Good morning, Bert. You lead the way.'

The man nodded. 'Right. Before we look at the door and the room, you might like to glance at the door to the fire escape over there so that you get a clear impression of the lie of the land.'

The bolt holding it shut was inside a box with a glass panel in its front and a metal hammer was hanging on a hook inside a wooden casing by its side.

'Do you know if it's checked regularly?' Fiona asked.

'They have a fire drill each term and it's opened then. It leads on to a metal staircase which extends to the two floors above and also to the ground.'

'What about access to the bolt for maintenance and the fire drills?'

'There's a lock at the side here, sir, and evidently there are three keys; the two women in charge here each have one and the third is kept in the college office in a large cabinet. Now, as for the door to the girl's room, you can see in this photograph that when we came on the scene the wood had been splintered where the house-mistress had used the base of the fire extinguisher to force her way in and we've secured it roughly with the hasp and padlock here. Shall we go in?' Once inside, he pointed to the inner aspect of the door. 'As you see, the original keyhole has been filled in and the door was secured on the inside by that bolt, which is a pretty flimsy affair and was torn out when the door was forced.'

'Any prints on it?'

'Just the girl's.'

The room was rectangular, approximately twelve feet by ten. As they stood in the middle of it, they saw the divan to their left standing alongside the wall which separated the room from the corridor. The head of the divan was against the other wall at right angles to it. Beside that was a small table with a lamp, a radio alarm clock and a book on it. Beyond the table was a basin with a medicine cabinet with a mirror set into it on the wall above it. Opposite the end of the divan was a wardrobe occupying the space between the door and the outside wall, into which was set a large sash window, which was secured by a catch in the fully closed position. There was a radiator beneath it.

'I see from the photograph that the window was just like that when you first examined it.'

'Yes, sir, and there were two sets of prints on that part of the frame, one was the girl's and it'll be up to you to decide whether to check the other against anyone else who might have had a legitimate reason for handling it, such as a cleaner or one of the other members of staff.'

Sinclair nodded. 'I'd like to have a closer look at it.'

Harris pushed the catch across and drew the bottom section up the short distance of no more than six inches until it hit the wooden stop. The upper section also had a stop on it, but that one allowed an open space of at least eighteen inches.

'The stops look as if they have been screwed in reasonably recently,' the man said. 'Perhaps it was done when the building was converted into a boarding house for the girls . . . litigation being what it is, I can't say I'm surprised. I made some enquiries about it and before this term, the room was used by one of the staff, a Miss Roberts.'

Sinclair nodded. He moved the chair from the desk nearby and climbed on to it, looking out of the window. Then he turned his attention to the desk which was set against the wall opposite the door. It had a set of drawers on its left side, which contained stationery, instruction manuals for the lap-top and printer both of which had been removed for study by the forensic people, some magazines and a folder containing a series of articles that had been cut out of newspapers and magazines. Further along this wall was a bookcase and an easy chair.

'Take a quick look through all that stuff, would you, Fiona, and then Bert can flesh out the details for us now that we've seen the general layout of the room?'

Sinclair was still standing there, wrapped in thought, when she finished inspecting the various papers, magazines and books.

'Find anything of interest? he asked.

'One or two things. There are three books on the early days of the transportations to Australia: 'The Fatal Shore'; one called '1788', by Watkin Tench and an account of Mary Bryant's escape from Botany Bay — she was the only woman to achieve that — all of them are obviously related to her project and there is a rough draft of the introduction, which has been printed out. I was flicking through the books and I came across this in the one about Mary Bryant,'

Fiona said, handing across the slip of paper.

''Mary never gave up, neither shall I',' Sinclair read out from the neat handwriting. 'Hmm, interesting. Do you know about Mary Bryant?' Fiona shook her head. 'She was the guiding force behind the escape and with her two small children and eight men in the Governor's cutter from Sydney, they rowed and sailed all the way to Timor. It's well over a thousand miles and, as I recall, only five of the adults, including Mary, survived and were pardoned on their return to England.'

'There is also an autographed photo of Ian Thorpe and there are also some newspaper cuttings about his triumphs in the Sydney and Athens Olympic Games.'

'The Australian swimmer?'

'That's right. There are also four novels; I'm not familiar with any of them except 'The Horse Whisperer', but from the blurbs on the others they all seem to have a feel-good theme with feisty girls overcoming ghastly early family circumstances and finding their way to romance and happiness. You know the sort of thing.'

Sinclair nodded. 'Right Bert, take us through the rest, would you?'

The man pulled a photograph out of his folder and held it up. 'To start with the girl. You can see that she was lying on her back, her eyes and mouth were open a fraction and she was wearing pyjamas. The house-mistress said in her statement that the girl had been lying on her front, with her head inclined to the left and the bedclothes were at the level of her neck and that she only moved them enough to satisfy herself that the girl was dead. Evidently she was able to see that the girl's left eye was open and that she wasn't breathing. As to the doctor, he turned the girl on to her back in order to listen for any heart beat, he felt for her pulse and shone his torch into her eyes. Dr Rawlings will be able to give you all the details about the pathological findings.'

'Right, perhaps now you'd take us through the various bits of furniture. How about the wardrobe to start with?'

'Forensic are still looking at the clothes that were in it, but they did find a half empty bottle of vodka in one of a pair of leather boots, hidden by some socks pushed into the top.'

Sinclair nodded. 'And the medicine cabinet?'

'Everything's been taken away for examination, but it's all itemised on the list you've got there, sir.'

The detective passed it across to Fiona. 'Any comments?'

'Brush, combs, nail scissors, small electric razor, athletes' foot powder, labelled plastic containers of paracetamol and an anti-histamine, jar of powder, lip salve, spare toothbrush, tube of toothpaste, bottle of shampoo and packets of tampons all seem innocuous enough. As far as the medicines are concerned, though, it obviously depends on the labels being correct.'

'Anything on the glass shelf?'

'Plastic mug with toothbrush and paste in it and soap and a flannel on the basin itself.'

'How about this bedside table and the drawer under the divan, Bert?'

'Beneath the divan is a large drawer; it's empty now, but you can see in the photo that is was full of clothes, mainly underwear, shirts and jumpers. Forensic are looking at them, but you've no doubt read that a packet of condoms was found hidden in the sleeve of one of them.'

The man pulled it open to show its dimensions and then moved to the small bedside table.

'The only things that have been moved are a glass jug and tumbler, both of which contained what looked like orange juice, but the lab are analysing them as well.'

'But where, one asks oneself,' Sinclair said, 'are the posters the knick-knacks, the photos, and the Ipod one would expect to find in a teenager's bedroom at a boarding-school? That large pin-board on the wall above the easy chair has even been provided, which, as you've already seen is empty except for a few drawing pins.'

Bert Harris nodded. 'My daughter's thirteen and you can't get into her room at home for all the clobber; it looks as if a group of vandals have just given it a through going over and that's when she's just tidied it up. It was one of the first things that struck me when I came in. All the clothes were neatly folded up, nothing was out of place and even the folders containing the project she'd had been working on were labelled and had been stacked neatly.'

'No sign of a suicide note?'

'No, sir, but I haven't yet heard the results of the examination of her computer.'

'Thanks, Bert, I think that's all for the time being. Any questions, Fiona?'

'No, thank you.'

★   ★   ★

After Sinclair had rung Miss Rainsford and made appointments to see the GP at the practice surgery and Derek Hammond in his office in London, the two detectives strolled across the games' field towards the swimming pool, where they were to meet Jo Roberts.

'I don't think there's much point in speculating further about the cause of Sophie's death until we've seen Rawlings on Friday; I know it looks like straight forward suicide, but I would be willing to bet that he has something up his sleeve, but we might as well get as clear a picture of the girl as we can; any views so far?'

'She certainly doesn't seem to have been exactly ideal material for a boarding-school,' Fiona said. 'It'll be interesting to see what her parents are like.'

'Yes. I'd like you to come with me to see Hammond in London and then we can tackle the mother later depending on how we get on with him.'

The house-mother was waiting for them in the lobby at the entrance to the gym complex and as she came forward towards them, smiling and with her hand outstretched, Sinclair was immediately struck by her slightly strutting, springy gait, so characteristic, he thought, of female gymnasts and ballet dancers. She was of average height and from what he was able to make out under her white tracksuit, she was stocky and there was no mistaking the strength of her fingers when she shook his hand. Despite the fact that there were flecks of grey in her black hair, which was styled, if one could call it that, in a very severe crew-cut, she looked to him to be no more than in her early thirties and was rather pretty, with a nice smile and dark brown eyes. From his own height of six foot two, he had immediately noticed the white, irregularly-shaped blaze on the crown of her head and, somewhat to his embarrassment, she immediately picked up the direction of his gaze and touched it with the tip of her forefinger.

'Legacy of a distinctly unpleasant event. My mother says it makes me look like a race horse, but I can't be bothered to keep dyeing it, particularly with all the swimming I do.'

'One of your stunts that went wrong?'

The woman smiled. 'So Margaret has been telling tales out of school, has she? Well, I'm sorry to have to disappoint you, but I didn't do the stunts myself, although I did have to demonstrate falls, climbs and high dives to the students when I was an instructor at the training school. No, in fact accidents are relatively rare in stunt work and I got mugged one evening in Bicester of all places. I finished up in the local hospital with a depressed fracture of the skull and my mobile phone and bag missing. I was lucky to get away without any brain damage, but was told on no account to run the risk of another head injury, which is why I decided to go into a more peaceful line of business. I would have done so anyway even without my injury; one does that sort of job whole-heartedly without fear and gives a hundred per cent, or one doesn't do it at all and anyway, advancing age was beginning to take its toll.'

'But still diving, are you?'

'Yes, but I stick to the springboard these days. No doubt you want to talk about Sophie. Why don't we go into the office? It's just over there.'

'How well did you know her?' Sinclair asked, when they were seated.

'As well as anyone here, I suppose. It was a thousand pities that she hadn't had a really good swimming coach when she was younger because she had an incredible natural talent. With me, it's all brute force, but she just seemed to glide on top of the water. It all looked so effortless, particularly her freestyle. I'm not in her league as a swimmer, except with strokes like the butterfly, which need more strength than she possessed, and, anyway, diving is my special skill in aquatic sports, but I was able to help her a bit by ironing out a few bad habits and her turns and starts weren't all that good.'

'Miss Rainsford was telling us that one of

the boys, also a keen swimmer, was quite friendly with her.'

'That would be Rob Preston. He's pretty good at water polo, but he's not much of a swimmer. The contrast between him and Sophie was much the same as that between a carthorse and a racehorse. She was all timing and fluency and he's all brute strength and . . . I was going to say ignorance, but that wouldn't be fair. He knows perfectly well that he hasn't got it, but I must say this for him, he is a trier and he does work hard. You need a lot of strength around the shoulders for water polo and so I get him to do weight training to build him up a bit more.'

'Was anything going on between them?'

'Sexually, you mean?'

'Yes.'

'I wouldn't have thought so. It's true that he couldn't take his eyes off her, but I think it was more like heroine worship, if I may put it that way. I did ask her if he was bugging her and she just shook her head and said: 'No, he's all right'. I could be wrong, of course, who knows what adolescents get up to these days?'

'We were surprised to see that there weren't any posters in Sophie's room and the one photo was of Ian Thorpe and that was in a folder with her project.'

'Yes, I know about that — she showed it to me. She had an absolute obsession about him; how nice he was, how good-looking and she was in raptures about his swimming technique — quite right, too, it is remarkable. She told me that she had videoed a lot of his races, which she kept at home and that she was terribly disappointed when he decided to retire at the end of 2006 as she was hoping to see him race at the Beijing Olympics on TV. She even went as far as to say that she would like to live in Australia.'

'What about her project?'

'That was coming along quite well, but she had got a bit side-tracked.'

'In what way?'

'She started off by wanting to write about the effect of the white colonisation of Australia on the aboriginal population, but during her reading, she found a reference to Mary Bryant and her escape from Botany Bay and asked me to get hold of a book about it, which I did for her on the internet from Amazon. For some reason, she identified with that and the fate of the convicts as a whole and I saw no reason to dissuade her — I was encouraged by the fact that she was showing initiative and independence of thought.'

'Did she ever tell you anything about her home life?'

'I tried asking, but didn't get anywhere at first and I saw no point in pressing her. It was obvious that Sophie wasn't going to fit in here right from the moment she arrived and when Miss Rainsford's attempt to get Charlotte to take her under her wing was clearly not working, she asked me if I'd take an interest in her, knowing that I would be seeing her on her own for swimming coaching. It took a bit of time, but I think it was the riding we did together that finally broke the ice. You see, I used to work for Mr Farr and his wife. He's a friend of Mr Hammond and they must both have thought it would be a good idea for Sophie to get away from the college occasionally at weekends and do some riding, which was one of her main hobbies at home. The Farrs, by their own admission, are not exactly in tune with difficult adolescent girls and that was why I was roped in.

'Don't get me wrong, it was no chore for me. I used to exercise one of their neighbours' horses when I lived there and riding was one of my skills at the stunt school. We were only able to go twice, but it seemed to relax Sophie and one afternoon, after swimming, she did tell me a bit about her problems. She said that her father had discovered that she was doing drugs, which was why she had been sent to boarding-school. She also told me that she had done some terrible things to get hold of the money to finance her habit. I found myself in a considerable dilemma. I had promised her that I wouldn't tell anyone about what she had said, which I felt I had to honour if I was to retain her trust, and she didn't specify the terrible things she claimed to have done, even though I pressed her. Certainly, there were no signs of her having had intravenous injections in the arms and I even wondered if she was romancing her past and seeking attention. Perhaps there were medical problems that her parents had kept from the school. I was concerned about these things, but even though she was rather flat and depressed when she first came here, she had begun to show real enthusiasm for her project, her swimming and the riding and I thought she was turning the corner.' The woman shook her head. 'She tended to get rather down when she had her period, but that had happened before and I didn't take it as anything serious. Perhaps I should have done, but not for one minute did I even consider the possibility that she might take her own life.'

'When was the last time that you saw her?'

'The day before she was found dead at our

usual morning swimming session.'

'Did she appear in any way to be unlike her normal self then?'

'She did seem a bit low, but, as I said, I put that down to no more than the after effects of her period.'

'Did you look in to see her last thing that evening?'

'No. When she left the pool, she told me that she was going to have a quiet day and an early night and I took her at her word. I'd already found that the more one treated her as a child, the more she behaved like one.'

Sinclair nodded. 'How did Sophie get on in the gym?'

'She wasn't really interested apart from the trampoline and only that when I told her that it wasn't only excellent training for diving, but for general co-ordination as well, which would benefit her swimming. In fact, as far as diving is concerned, the springboard is the only one we have here and that's only allowed to be used by the pupils under supervision. They're too scared about litigation for anything more elaborate and that also applies to the gym. As I'm not a qualified instructor, they're not prepared to risk the use of any of the potentially dangerous pieces of apparatus such as the beam, the horizontal and the asymmetric bars and they're all locked away at present. I am allowed to instruct on the trampoline and use it whenever I want to myself — that and the springboard have been special interests of mine for a long time — but again I have to lock any moveable apparatus away in the storeroom at all other times. The trampoline's a bit of a drag as it's so heavy, but one of the ground staff is always prepared to give me a hand with it.'

'Working in this place must be a bit different from being involved with stunts.'

She smiled. 'It certainly is, but I'm getting into it and I really enjoy it now.'

'How did you hear about this post?'

'When I gave up working at the stunt school, I managed to get a job in a health club, that's how I first met Mrs Farr and she persuaded me to become her personal trainer with a bigger salary than I was earning at the club. She's a lot younger than her husband and used to be a dancer. She would be the first to admit that she had let herself go a bit and as she wanted to get back to it, I was taken on to get her into shape. Unfortunately, after about a year, her husband hit the financial buffers pretty hard and I had to go. Mr Farr's on the Board here, he heard about this job becoming vacant and with this new complex having just been finished and without the funds to staff it, I imagine they thought they might kill two birds with one stone and at least get a swimming and gym instructor on the cheap.'

'That sounds uncommonly like exploitation to me.'

'And it did to me, too — the pay was a bit of a joke — but I did get my keep and Mr Manners was quite open about it right from the start and indicated that he would do what he could to get me a bigger salary as a gym and swimming instructor later on.'

'And did he succeed?'

'Yes, my pay was upped at the start of this term.'

'Good for you. Well, thank you for your help.'

'No problem. Any time.'

★　★　★

'What did you make of her?' Sinclair asked as they drove towards the GP's surgery.

'A bit of a tough nut, but seemed straight forward enough to me. She's obviously gay.'

Sinclair hadn't failed to notice the way the young woman had looked at Fiona when they were shaking hands. There had been nothing overt about it, but the subtle appraisal had been made none the less. He also hadn't missed the almost imperceptible tightening of the woman's lips when she saw the faint flush that had come into his colleague's cheeks.

'I agree, but we shouldn't read too much into that. The teaching profession wouldn't be able to function were it not for the likes of her. I remember very well one of the masters at my prep school. I don't believe for one moment that he ever did anything physical about it, but he just happened to like small boys. That gave him patience with them, an interest, enthusiasm and an understanding that none of the others could begin to match. Of course, real paedophiles must be dealt with, but if that is carried to extremes, inevitably witch hunts result and, as is all too evident now, school authorities and teachers have become defensive both with regard to that and litigation; there are hardly any men in primary schools any longer. Parents are also expecting standards of safety and supervision on school trips that they don't practise themselves and that's going to kill off adventure and any form of risk taking. You don't agree?'

Fiona didn't reply straight away, staring straight ahead through the windscreen.

'I think it's easy to believe that things were better in the past, but I'm quite sure that very often they weren't.'

'That's perfectly true, but that doesn't alter

my view that the 'blame culture' is a pernicious trend.'

Dr McIntosh's surgery was on the edge of the nearby country town and the receptionist showed them into his consulting room. He was a stocky, grandfatherly-looking man who, Sinclair judged, must be well into his sixties. He had a thick head of white hair, a matching moustache and a pronounced Scottish accent.

'This is a very attractive facility,' Sinclair said after the introductions had been made.

'Aye. It's only been open for five years and, believe it or not, I was against the notion when it was first mooted. I'd got used to working in my own house and I couldn't be doing with rosters, practice nurses, reception-ists, computers and all that stuff. I was quite wrong; my way was all very well when general practice was so much more personal and the patients were on one's side in a way that a great many are no longer. If anything goes wrong now, it's automatically assumed that it's someone's fault and those affected are straight off to one of those no win, no fee characters. It makes my blood boil when I see their sanctimonious adverts on TV. The need for support has become a necessity for GPs and that's what I get here. I have the chance to discuss problems with my colleagues merely by stepping into the next room, there are receptionists to calm down the disgruntled and at my age I'm no longer up to the twenty-four hour cover I used to give to my patients.

'It's true that as a result of group practices and far fewer home visits, patient care has become much less personal, but the days of the single-handed practitioner are over. Apart from anything else, the wives are no longer the same breed as my Ella and when she died I either joined a group or gave up.'

'What about the college?'

'Now that's something I've really enjoyed over the last thirty years.'

'What exactly has it involved?'

'A good deal more than minor medical questions. Soon after I started, I took on sex education and advice. That was long before it became fashionable and the problem with drugs didn't exist in that sort of environment. It soon became known that I could be trusted with confidences, whatever they were, and in that I was backed up by the headmaster, Guy Manners, a man for whom I have the greatest respect.'

'What about the advent of the girls?'

'That has not proved so easy. You see, I'm sure I don't need to tell you that the balance of power between males and females has altered and a lot of the trust that used to exist has now gone. As a result, although I hated having to do it, I soon saw that the only sensible course was to get one of my female colleagues to take on their care, including the counselling, before there was a complaint. I have even given up looking after the girls' purely physical illnesses, apart, that is, from the times when my colleague is ill or on holiday.'

'Did either you or your colleague see Sophie Hammond for any reason during the short time she was at the college?'

'Dr Peters did the routine medical examinations that all the new pupils have at the beginning of the autumn term and the girl was also a member of the group to which she gave a talk about sex soon after their arrival. Immediately after I heard about Sophie Hammond's death, I did ask her if she had found anything unusual about her and the answer was no apart from the fact that she seemed more shy about her body than the other new girls.'

'Who asked you to go in when Sophie was found dead?'

'Guy Manners. I wouldn't even have done that had Dr Peters not been on maternity leave. Her baby's expected any day now and as she's had a bit of a problem with her blood pressure, she's been away for a couple of weeks already and has to spend most of her time in bed. Even then, I thought it wise for Miss Rainsford to accompany me into the girl's room. I have Harold Shipman to thank for believing that such a course of action would be prudent.'

'What exactly did you do?'

'She was lying on her front with her head turned to the left and I had to turn her over and pull down the bedclothes a bit to make quite sure that she was indeed dead as Miss Rainsford had said. I listened for heart sounds, felt for the temporal, carotid and radial pulses, checked her pupils, which I found to be fixed and dilated, and looked for any sign of respiration by holding the pocket mirror I have in my bag in front of her mouth. An overdose seemed to me to be the most likely cause of death, but I know enough about forensic medicine to understand that the experts are best left with the field as undisturbed as possible.'

Sinclair nodded. 'I'm sure that Dr Rawlings would agree with that.'

Dr McIntosh smiled. 'I have not the slightest doubt of it and I feel sure that he disapproved of the little I felt I had to do. He gave a talk to our local medical society a year or so ago and he made that very point to us. I was going to say forcefully, but that would be a major understatement.'

* * *

The granite slab on the side of the tall building in the City of London merely said 'Hammond Enterprises' and the two detectives went through the revolving door and walked up to the desk in the lobby. The pretty, red-haired young woman wearing a green suit looked up and smiled as they approached.

'How may I help you, sir?'

Wonders will never cease, Sinclair thought; for once someone had said 'may' instead of 'can'.

He gave her a smile. 'Inspector Sinclair and DC Campbell to see Mr Hammond.'

'Yes, sir. He's expecting you both.'

Clive Hammond was wearing a dark suit and a Hawks' Club tie and advanced to greet them as they were shown into his room by his personal assistant, who had met them as they came out of the lift. The large room had a picture window set into the wall behind the desk and through it Sinclair caught a glimpse of a spectacular view of St Paul's. The man, who appeared to be in his late forties, was a shade under six feet tall and heavily built with thick brown hair flecked with grey, he was deeply tanned.

It was the detective's experience that people in Hammond's situation were usually nervous and couldn't stop talking; the man, though, did the exact opposite, sitting quite relaxed in the black leather chair and saying nothing as Sinclair expressed his condolences.

'I'm afraid that the pathologist hasn't finished his tests yet, but we are going to see him tomorrow and I should have news for you then.'

'Why the delay?'

'I won't know until I've seen him, but it's not uncommon for the analysis of specimens to take some time.'

'What sort of specimens?'

'Blood tests. I think you know that alcohol was found in her room and we also have to check for that and drugs as well.'

The man nodded. 'Manners mentioned the possibility of that to me and I have to confess that when he rang me with the appalling news that morning, it confirmed my worst fears. Let me explain. Sophie always was a strange child, solitary and rather withdrawn, not making friends easily and disliking parties, but it was only a year or so ago that I began to have suspicions that she might be taking drugs. She started to become even more difficult, being sullen and uncommunicative and spending a lot of time in her room. At first I just put it down to adolescence and thought she would grow out of it in time, but then she stopped speaking to us altogether. It was much worse for my wife; although I looked upon Sophie as my daughter with no reservations whatever, I was not her natural father. She must have been about five when I married her mother and adopted her and I'm sorry to say that things never went that well between us and latterly, there was a considerable change in her behaviour for the worse.

'Celia and I decided to tackle the form mistress at the local day school which she was attending at that time. All she would say was that Sophie was shy and young for her age, but that she was getting on very well with her work and they had every confidence that she would blossom socially in due course. Outside school, her main interest was swimming, but even that was something of a concern, because she used to do it on her own in our pool. When she was little I arranged for her to have lessons and used to take her to the local pool myself — that was before we had one of our own — and when it became clear that she was definitely good at it, I tried to encourage her to join a club and take part in competitive events, but she wouldn't, preferring to practise by herself. During the holidays, my wife told me that virtually the only times she left the house were to go to one of the local riding schools on her bike. I say appeared because, although I am not exactly proud of the fact, last summer, I followed her one day on my mountain bike, which I use to keep in shape. One of the things that alerted me was that despite having told us that she was going riding, she wasn't wearing the kit that she normally did for that. Anyway, my hunch proved correct; she didn't go riding, she cycled up to the station, locked her bike up and took the train to London. On my return, I searched her room and even though I found nothing, I still wasn't reassured — there were so many other places where she might have hidden the stuff.'

'What did you do then?'

'I tackled her when she came back, saying that I was extremely concerned about her and whatever it was, I would do anything in my power to help. I asked where she had been and if she was taking drugs and she just refused to answer. What was I going to do? Celia is prone to bad depressions and I couldn't risk sharing my fears with her and I couldn't face putting an enquiry agent on to Sophie. So in the end, I decided that I would ask Guy Manners if, as a favour, he would take her as a boarder at Sandford College. I had the hope — it seems naïve now — that in a closed community like that, she might be able to get herself together, particularly as they had a first-rate swimming pool there and a female instructor who might take a special interest in her.'

'How did Sophie react to the suggestion?'

'I was expecting, if not tears, at least some emotion, but all I got was silence and to my surprise she went along with all the arrangements without protest.'

'Did you tell Manners about your drug fears?'

'No, I didn't think that would be fair to Sophie if I was wrong, but I did say that I was worried about her, that she seemed unhappy for no reason that I had been able to discover. I suspected, however, that she might have been bullied at her other school. He promised that the house-mistress would keep a careful eye on her and keep me informed of her progress. He did just that and I was quite encouraged; he told me that she had settled in well, had impressed the swimming instructor with her ability and dedication and was working hard at a project. The dreadful news came as the most terrible shock. Let me say straight away that I'm not blaming the school for this in any way; I should have realised just how depressed Sophie was and that failure is something I shall have to shoulder — I can tell you that that will be no easy task.'

'Did she have any sexual problems as far as you were aware?'

'I'm afraid I can't help you there. Latterly I found it impossible to talk to Sophie about anything, let alone that. I do know that my wife went through the mechanics of it all with her, but no more than that. She did tell me that she had tried to broach the topic more recently but that the shutters had come down. I also know that the subject was tackled at both her day school and Sandford College, but I have no idea how well it was done. I am sorry not to be more helpful, but adolescent sexuality, particularly in girls, is a closed book to me.'

'If, as seems possible, she did take an overdose, would you have any objection to one of our experts looking at her bedroom at home and examining her computer and mobile phone if she had those there?'

'Any particular reason?'

'Just that we must make every effort to find her supplier, if indeed she had one. I suppose she might have made contacts on the internet.'

Hammond nodded. 'I see. No, I don't have any problem with that.'

'We would also like to have a word with your wife.'

'I expected you'd ask this and from my point of you I would welcome it, I can't, of course, answer for her. I would request you, though, to take it gently — Celia is a very nervous person and terribly upset at the moment.'

Sinclair nodded. 'I was thinking of getting DC Campbell here to see her in the first instance. She has had experience in the drug field, particularly as far as adolescents are concerned, and that has meant a lot of contact with parents.'

The man looked at Fiona and smiled. 'That's an excellent idea; I'm sure it will reassure Celia.'

'Doubtless you'd like to be present when we come as well. Would this coming weekend be possible for you, say Saturday afternoon?'

'Would it be asking too much for you to make it Sunday. I have a meeting on Saturday and, although at a pinch I could reschedule it, it would cause major inconvenience to a lot of people.'

'No, you mustn't do that, Sunday would be

fine as far as I am concerned. Fiona?'

Hammond looked towards her and when she nodded said: 'Would about three p.m. suit you both?'

'Yes, thank you. We have your home address — the college gave it to us.'

5

'Inspector Sinclair and Detective Constable Campbell to see you, Dr Rawlings.'

'There's no need to shout, Miss Ryle, I'm not deaf, at least not yet, nor am I so blind that I'm unable to recognise our visitors. Coffee and the Bath Olivers, if you please, Miss Ryle and not just three of them, I'm feeling distinctly peckish and Miss Campbell here needs building up. How are you, my dear, quite recovered from your injuries I trust?'

'Yes, thank you, and very happy to be back on the job.'

'On the job? You don't mean that . . . '

'Not that particular job I'm sorry to have to tell you.'

Rawlings let out a loud guffaw. 'Haven't lost your sense of humour, I'm glad to hear, which is more than can be said for a lot of your sex, not least the otherwise inestimable Miss Ryle.' Fiona glanced round and to her relief saw that the man's secretary had gone and that the door was shut, but inevitably he had noticed her reaction and gave her one of his vulpine grills. 'It's a commodity you must need in your job what with that Baines case and now this one.'

At that moment, there was a sound at the door and Sinclair got up and held it open for the secretary, who came in wheeling a trolley.

' ''Some say that the age of chivalry is past, that the spirit of romance is dead. The age of chivalry is never past, so long as there is wrong left unredressed.' Pretty apposite, don't you think, Miss Campbell?'

Fiona nodded, not having the faintest idea what the man was talking about and hoping that her response was the correct one.

'Nobody reads Kingsley these days, more's the pity. Miss Ryle!' he suddenly rasped. 'Why is it that I fail to see the sugar lumps and my esteemed grandmother's silver tongs?'

'Your physician, Dr Rawlings . . . '

'Just as I thought. Give me someone plump and cheerful with a bit of meat on them, rather than that lean and hungry Cassius-like figure, who's invariably a prophet of gloom and as miserable as sin. The wretched fellow lives on a diet of muesli, yogurt and spinach; serve him right if he dropped dead of the heart attack he's always threatening me with.'

'Dr Rawlings!'

The man wasn't the least abashed by his secretary's horrified expression and gave a loud chortle. 'The sugar, if you please, Miss Ryle, and look sharp, would you? We have important matters to attend to.'

When they had been served with the coffee and the secretary had departed, Rawlings opened the folder in front of him and took out several sheets of paper.

'You do pick 'em, don't you, Sinclair? This girl, Sophie Hammond, certainly packed a good deal into her sixteen years. Firstly, there were some sachets of high grade cocaine buried in a large pot of talcum powder in the cupboard under the basin, she had a blood alcohol of 80 mg per 100 ml and clear evidence of flunitrazepam in her urine. Miss Campbell?'

'The trade name is rohypnol and the press like to call it the 'date rape' drug.'

'What a mine of information you are, to be sure! There you are, Sinclair, that's what sugar can do for you. The drug was also present in the small amount of orange juice left in the glass, as was alcohol, which no doubt came from the vodka bottle. Tablets of the rohypnol were in a bottle labelled as piriton, a mild antihistamine.'

'What about fingerprints?' Sinclair asked.

'The girl's were the only ones found on the tumbler, flask, vodka bottle and the various items in the cabinet under the basin.'

'The rohypnol doesn't make sense to me. Surely the girl wouldn't have been using it as a night sedative.'

'No indeed. It is about six times as potent as other benzodiazepines of which valium is perhaps the best known, but it does give people a high, particularly if taken with alcohol.'

'Were the blood levels of the mixture enough to have killed her?'

'As always, my dear Sinclair, you have put your finger squarely on the button. No, I don't think so, even though others would almost certainly dispute both that and my view that she was almost certainly suffocated.'

'Suffocated?' Sinclair said. 'By someone or accidentally?'

'The former.'

'But she was found in a room with the door bolted on the inside and the only window, one of the sash variety, was securely fastened on the inside.'

'That's your problem, my dear fellow; I can only tell you that I believe she was suffocated by someone. You may not know that I did a detailed study of so-called cot deaths and how to differentiate them from deliberate suffocation and there is no real doubt in my mind, even if there might be in others.'

'Condoms were found in her belongings, as

I am sure you know,' Sinclair said, 'but were there any physical findings to confirm recent or past sexual activity?'

'There certainly were, front and back, to put it as delicately as I am able. I'll go into the evidence if you like and I have some photographs . . . '

'I'm quite happy to take your word for it.'

Rawlings let that one pass, although Sinclair didn't fail to notice the twitch of his lips and glint in his eye.

'Too much to expect that there was any DNA evidence, I suppose,' Fiona said.

'Hah, I rather thought that your DNA expert wouldn't let that one pass, Sinclair. Alas, no, neither on her, inside her, fore or aft, nor were there semen stains on her night or bedclothes. There were no other signs of any recent physical activity in that department, either. Apart from what I've already mentioned, she was perfectly healthy and to save your asking, she had never been pregnant, nor was there any evidence of long standing cocaine usage such as damage to the nasal passages which may result from prolonged use of that drug.'

'How strongly will you be able to pitch the suffocation angle in your report to the coroner?'

'Not very, I'm afraid. The changes were not

dramatic and I know one or two of my colleagues would be quite capable of saying that her death was accidental and that the findings were consistent with her having rolled on to her front when heavily asleep under the influence of alcohol and the drugs she had taken and that her airways might have been obstructed by the pillow. Yes, I am aware that she was indeed found in that position. Anyway, my opinion is hardly likely to cut much ice with our friend Rodney Twyford; decisive conclusions are hardly his strong suit.'

Sinclair did know. The coroner was, in his own, and indeed most other people's view, a frightful old woman and if he could express doubt and bring in an open verdict, he would.

'I see, but strictly entre nous, you have no real doubt that she was suffocated?'

'None at all. Any other questions?'

'That of possible suicide is bound to be raised, although I have doubts about that, too, not least because of the note that was found in a book in her room.'

Sinclair explained about that and the girl's interest in Mary Bryant and Rawlings nodded. 'Any comments Miss Campbell?'

'Have you ever come across anyone committing suicide with a mixture of rohypnol and alcohol?'

'No, I haven't. You see, the former isn't used as a sleeping pill because it also produces confusion and impairment of memory for recent events, but young women have died from its effects when it has been administered by men, often in alcoholic drinks, for the purpose of non-consensual sexual activity. Another point is that its employment as a recreational drug in young people must be very unusual — I have already alluded to the fact that it can create a high and I have also read that it has been used for such purposes, but I've never come across it personally and it's most unlikely that a young girl would be using it that way; glue sniffing, ecstasy and speed are some of the drugs most commonly employed if such an end is desired by that age group.'

'What about the alcohol in this case?'

'It was in the orange juice as you have no doubt already deduced and her blood level, although not all that elevated, was high enough to have enhanced the effects of the rohypnol.'

'Would anyone realise they were drinking alcohol if, say vodka, had been present in that concentration in orange juice?' Sinclair asked.

'That's an interesting point and there has been reliable research done on that subject.

Two groups of students in the USA were told that they were going to be given various tests some of them with and some without alcohol in orange juice. The ones who thought that they were drinking the alcohol mixture did significantly worse than those who thought they were taking the pure juice. In fact, they had been misled into believing the opposite of what had been given to them. The point of the exercise was to show that psychological factors were playing the most important part in that particular instance, but it also demonstrated that it was possible to give that amount of alcohol without the subjects being reliably aware of it and the levels used were higher than the one I found in Sophie Hammond.'

'What state would she have been in with the level of the rohypnol you found?'

'Certainly deeply unconscious, but not, I think, in danger of death. Good luck to you, I fear you're going to need it by the look of things. Don't hesitate to ask if you have any further queries — I find this case more than a little intriguing.'

★ ★ ★

After Celia Hammond had taken her husband's coffee to him as he lay on the lounger by the pool with the paper, as he always did on a Sunday morning when he was at home, she sat in the drawing-room staring at the painting on the wall opposite. She had been feeling anxious and uneasy ever since Clive had told her that the police were coming to see them that afternoon and her husband noticed it at once.

'There's no need to worry, my dear,' he had said, 'they always have to make thorough enquires in a situation like this.'

She was worried, though; if Sophie really had been on drugs and had taken an overdose, either deliberately or by accident, had she herself been in any way responsible? Her mind went back to what had happened all those years ago.

★ ★ ★

Bill Clarke had been a bright, grammar-school boy, but had got in with a rough crowd, missed the chance of going to college and before long was in and out of one dodgy job after another. He had worked for a shady second-hand car dealer, sold stolen goods from a stall at the local street market and then tried his luck at being a door-to-door salesman, peddling kitchen accessories. That was how he came to meet Rosie Butler. He didn't know then that she was the daughter of a man who ran a successful bookmaking business, but what he did know was that although it might take a bit of time, she was ripe for the plucking. It didn't turn out to be quite so simple as he had expected; she proved reluctant, she had to be primed with quite a few drinks, he got careless himself and the inevitable happened. She was frightened of what her parents would do if they found out and, when it became impossible to hide her pregnancy any longer, it was too late to do anything about it. Fred Butler was not a violent man, but he had plenty of violent friends and associates on whom he could call whenever the need arose and it was made only too clear to young Bill Clarke that unless he did the right thing by Rosie, his features would be rearranged or worse.

The marriage was a failure right from the start. Rosie had a difficult pregnancy and wanted nothing to do with the man who had been responsible for it either during or after the baby girl was born. She called her daughter Celia after the actress Celia Johnson in the film 'Brief Encounter', which she had seen at a cinema. To make matters worse Rosie became severely depressed. Had Clarke been able to find consolation elsewhere, he might have been able to accept the situation, but his father-in-law kept a watchful eye on things, there were more warnings after he had hit her a few times and he took out his frustration by drinking, hating both his wife and the baby.

When Fred Butler died suddenly from a heart attack and Bill Clarke took over the betting shop, things became easier for a time. He had money, his father-in-law's old associates had either melted away or lost interest in him and he found consolation in a string of girls, who were only too ready to show their appreciation for the generosity of his presents.

Throughout her childhood, Celia managed to avoid the consequences of her father's drunken attacks of violent temper, for the most part, by making herself scarce and keeping a low profile. The same could not be said of her mother, who would often have a split lip, or have to cover up bruises. Celia studied hard and did very well at school and by the time she was sixteen she was encouraged by her teachers to stay on, she was told she was certainly capable of getting into a university if she kept up the good work. Bill Clarke would have none of it. She was going to leave school, get a job and contribute to the family finances. He even found one for her, in the pub which he used to frequent himself and where he and the landlord, who was a friend of his, would be able to keep an eye on her. She hated it there; the regulars were a bunch of loud-mouthed idiots, who were always making obscene jokes and having a go at the Asians and blacks, none of whom were stupid enough to come within a mile of the place. They were also for ever making coarse remarks about what they used to call her 'assets' — but only when her dad wasn't within earshot, of course.

She stood it for eighteen months and then found herself a job at one of the good hotels near the airport. What made this possible was that she got talking to the owner of a hardware store, who went to the pub from time to time and had taken a liking to her. He heard about her plans to better herself and he offered to give her a reference. The man felt sorry for her, having no time for her father, and, as he was on the local council, his letter carried a good deal of weight.

Her father had been predictably furious, but for once she stood up to him, not being afraid to say that she had the support of one of her grandfather's heavies, who still had considerable influence locally. That wasn't strictly true — she had heard about the man from her grandmother, who had told her once about the way he had protected her mother after her grandfather had died and she was able to drop hints about that. Her father ranted and raged for a time, but underneath it all he was a weak individual and when he heard that her pay would be much better, he used it as an opportunity to insist on taking a bigger cut for her keep. This was both grossly unfair and a joke — she did a great deal more around the house than both her parents put together.

Celia Clarke had been at the hotel for about three months when early one evening, when she was alone in the residents' bar polishing some glasses, the man walked in. The hotel was used by a number of the airlines serving the airport and the crews were a familiar sight there, but she had never seen anyone looking like him. He was so smart in his uniform, so good-looking, with a few streaks of silver in his thick, dark hair and his slight foreign accent added to his glamorous aura.

He ordered a gin and tonic, offered her whatever she would like herself and then sat down on one of the bar stools. A good twenty minutes went by before anyone else came in and she discovered that he was called Klaus, that he was the captain of an aircraft and was working for Lufthansa and that he was a widower. He asked her about her family and then entertained her with stories about the exotic places he had been to, the famous people he had met and some of the exciting and strange events that had occurred during his flights.

A fault having developed in one of the engines of his aircraft, he stayed for three nights at the hotel until the plane had been repaired and each evening, he came into the bar to have a chat with her. She hadn't believed him when he said that he was looking forward to seeing her again when next he was in Birmingham, but he had and invited her out to dinner at a restaurant on her evening off.

Like so many young women of her background at the time, she was woefully ignorant about sex and when he suggested that it would set the seal on a memorable evening if she went back with him to his room for a nightcap, she wasn't frightened, merely excited at spending more time alone with such a nice and attractive man. She was feeling giggly and happy when they got there and the eagerly anticipated kisses and cuddles soon turned into a great deal more than that.

He was full of praise for her looks, how bright and pretty she was and how beautifully formed and how desirable. Like many girls of her generation, particularly the less worldly ones, whose sole sex instruction had been through furtive conversations with friends at school, she was frightened that it would hurt her and that she wouldn't enjoy it, but Klaus reassured her about that, telling her that that might be the case with an overeager young fellow, who wouldn't be able to take his time and not have the patience to look after her needs, but not with a man like him, whose greatest pleasure was to do just that.

All the time, with gentle caresses and whispered words of praise and encouragement, her excitement was building and when it reached a crescendo, it was as if a dam had burst and she lost control, only just aware that she had cried out. He didn't turn away from her when it was over, either, holding her in a warm embrace until she fell asleep. If it had been lovely the first time, it was even better the second early the following morning, slower and less urgent. Afterwards, when lying completely relaxed in the bath, she had never felt so happy. Even then, there was more to come, the large breakfast that Klaus had ordered through room service, being more than enough for both of them.

By the following afternoon, she had come to believe that it had been a dream and that she would never see him again, but he did come back into the bar the next day and after he had explained that he was being moved on to a different route and wouldn't be able to see her again, he gave her a beautiful diamond brooch, explaining that it had belonged to his wife and that he wanted her to have it because she had restored that part of his life that he thought he would never experience again and that he would never forget her.

As for her, Celia never had bad memories of Klaus, not even when she discovered that one of the many myths she had believed, that it was not possible to get pregnant the first time one did it, proved as false as her fear that it would necessarily be painful. Even if termination of the pregnancy had been an issue, which it wasn't because firstly she was too frightened of her father to tell him or her mother what had happened until it was too late, she would never have agreed to it. She was proud of the fact that the father of the baby was such a fine man as Klaus.

As for her own father, predictably he made no allowance for the fact that exactly the same thing had happened to him and her mother, clearly believing that there was one law for him and quite a different one for her. She was turned out of the house, being well aware that she had been lucky to get away without being on the receiving end of a beating. She had an aunt, her mother's sister, in London and the woman took her in, but that didn't last, because once her baby, Sophie, had been born, her aunt's husband began to complain and Celia knew perfectly well that it was only a matter of time before she would be told to leave.

Things took a turn for the better when she managed to get a job as a hostess at a night club and was able to share a small flat with a girl who also had a baby and who also worked at the club during the day as a cleaner. It wasn't much of a place, but it suited them both. The girl looked after Sophie while she was at work at night and Celia she did the same for the other baby during the day.

Her life was turned round when, three years later, Clive Hammond saw her at the club and offered her a job at his casino. He was looking for a croupier and when he found that she was good with figures and was quick to understand the various games when they had been explained to her, he had her properly trained, arranged for her to have lessons with a voice teacher to get rid of her Birmingham accent and speak appropriately for a job like that and her hair was restyled and she was supplied with elegant dresses so that she looked the part.

She was half expecting to have to repay Clive in the way she knew that girls in her position so often did, but he was always very much the perfect gentleman with her and even though he used to take her out to dinner and the theatre, he never made the slightest move in that direction. She was often to wonder later why he had wanted to marry her, because he never showed much interest in her sexually. If she had stayed with Klaus, she knew that that side of life would have been very different, but who was she to complain when her husband was so unfailingly kind and generous towards her and she had all the material comforts. His penthouse flat, where they started their married life was quite something, but it couldn't compare with the new house he had had built, particularly as he had discussed the design and decor with her at every stage of its construction. She supposed that some men like him, who worked so hard and for such long hours, just didn't have the energy for the sex bit as well. After a time, it didn't bother her either and she had her memories.

She never told Clive about Klaus, the main reason being that she believed that he would either think that she had made the whole thing up, or else got it from a story in some silly magazine. At times, she had hardly been able to believe it herself and so she said that one of the local boys had got her drunk, taken advantage of her inexperience and ignorance and that, as a result, she had been thrown out of the house by her father. Clive had been sympathetic and understanding about that, too, and never mentioned it again.

The one real sadness in her life had been Sophie's attitude to Clive. The little girl was five years old when they got married and to start with she seemed happy with him, but as she got older that all changed and she started to withdraw from him despite the fact that he had tried everything possible to be a real father to her. Had it been her own fault, Celia wondered? She liked and respected her husband, but she had never really loved Clive, not in the way she had loved Klaus, even though she had only known the German for such a short time. Had Sophie sensed that? Why hadn't she told Sophie about Klaus, either? She had thought about it so many times and had intended to do so once Sophie was old enough to understand, but by then she was caught in the web of the lie she had told Clive and hadn't the courage to go back on that, particularly after she had even asked his advice early in their marriage about the best time to explain to Sophie that she was illegitimate. 'The truth is always best in situations like this,' he had said, 'but I think it would be wise to wait until she is older unless, of course, she should ever ask you directly.'

She had decided to leave it until Sophie was eighteen, but then, quite out of the blue, when she was fifteen, Sophie said to her one day:

'Clive isn't my real father, is he?'

Taken by surprise and having no time to think, Celia suddenly decided to tell her the whole truth. Tears and recriminations she would have understood, but not the unblinking stare that followed after she had finished.

'I know it must be hard for you to understand, but Clive has tried so hard to be a proper father to you. Couldn't you at least show him some appreciation for all that he's done to help you with your swimming and everything else?'

Sophie never took her eyes off her mother's face as she tried to explain how difficult it had been for her and Clive to try to understand why she was so unhappy and if only she would tell them what was wrong, whatever it was, they would do everything possible to put it right.

'Why didn't you tell me about my real father long ago?'

'We both thought at first we should wait until you were old enough to understand and then when you started to withdraw into yourself, I . . . '

Celia had felt a tear start to roll down her cheek and then when, without saying a word, Sophie got up from the sofa and walked out of the room, her fragile control had snapped and she began to sob uncontrollably.

★   ★   ★

Celia was still staring at the wall opposite, lost in her thoughts, when Maria, the Italian housekeeper knocked on the door and came in.

'Lunch will be ready in about fifteen minutes, madam.'

'Thank you, Maria, I'll tell Mr Hammond.'

When they sat down together for their meal, her husband looked across the table at her and smiled.

'Don't worry, dear. I met the policewoman, who's going to have a chat to you, in London and she's not a threatening person at all; in fact, she seemed rather shy. She'll want to know about Sophie and you must just tell her everything. After all, we've discussed it often enough ourselves and if she was taking drugs, it's only right that the police should do their utmost to find those responsible for supplying her.'

Celia nodded. 'Yes, I do see that, Clive. I'll be all right.'

★   ★   ★

On that fine late October Sunday afternoon, the trees on the main road running south out of Esher were looking their best, the sun bringing out the autumn tints.

'My goodness,' Sinclair said, 'this takes me back. I haven't been down this road since I was at a prep school near Cobham and we used to go riding not all that far from here — lovely spot, isn't it? Ah, here we are, it's to the left down there.'

The Hammond's house was like those nearby, being modern, detached and in roughly half an acre of immaculately tended land. It didn't look more than a few years old and was built in mellow brick. There was a double garage on one side and against the other had been constructed a substantial extension, with large areas of glass set into the wall facing the lawn. While Bert Harris was getting his gear out of the boot, Sinclair and Fiona walked a few paces towards it.

'As I thought, there's a pool in there and it must be all of twenty-five metres long,' he said.

'All right for some.'

Sinclair grinned at her. 'Go on, you'd hate it in a place like this — I know I would.'

A dark-complexioned woman in her

103

thirties, wearing a uniform, answered their ring. 'Please to wait here? I fetch Mr Hammond', she said in heavily accented English.

The man appeared a few moments later. He was dressed in slacks, a dark blue blazer and a silk cravat and shook hands with all three of them.

'Right,' he said, crisply, 'I'll take you and your man upstairs, Sinclair, and perhaps Miss Campbell would like to have a chat with my wife.' The man gave Fiona a warm smile. 'It's this way.'

He made a gesture with his hand towards the door to their right and opened it for her.

'Don't get up, dear,' Hammond said as he walked into the room. 'The Inspector, his technical assistant and I are just going upstairs and Miss Campbell here will keep you company. You might like to show her the garden.'

'I would enjoy that,' Fiona said, when the three men had left the room and the door had been closed. 'From what I have seen already, it looks absolutely lovely, as does your house.'

'Do you really think so, dear?'

'Yes, I do.'

The woman looked very young to be the mother of a sixteen year old girl, but as soon as she tried to smile, Fiona realised that the lack of lines in her face was due more to botox, or expensive and subtle face lifts, than nature. She had beautifully cut hair, which must have cost her a fortune and was wearing an extremely elegant light beige dress.

'Would you like to have a quick look around downstairs as well as the garden?'

'Oh, yes please.'

Fiona wasn't feigning her enthusiasm, she had never even been in a place like this, let alone seen round one. The woman brightened visibly and the tour began. There was the dining-room, with the enormous mahogany table and ten chairs round it, the eighteenth-century longcase grandfather clock and the painting of St Mark's Square above the mantelpiece.

'It's a Canaletto. Clive was so pleased to get it at Sotheby's many years ago. I daren't tell you how much it cost, but he told me that its value would appreciate greatly in time and, of course, he was right. Clive knows all about things like that, you see. I hadn't realised that there are practically no Canalettos in Venice — they were all sold to wealthy Europeans doing the Grand Tour. Rather sad that, don't you think?'

It was almost as if she had forgotten about her daughter as, after a quick look at the state-of-the-art kitchen, they went back into the living-room and through the French windows.

'Sophie must have enjoyed this lovely pool,' Fiona said.

Quite suddenly the woman's face crumpled and she burst into tears.

Fiona put her arms round her. 'I'm so sorry, I didn't mean to upset you like that.'

It only took only a few moments for the woman to recover her composure and after she had dabbed her cheeks with a tissue from the box on the table by one of the loungers at the poolside, she led the way back into the drawing-room.

'Clive said it was better for me not to think or talk about Sophie too much, but I don't think that's right, do you?'

'No I don't. Whatever people say, men and women cope with tragedies like this in different ways and what may be right for someone with an unemotional temperament like your husband may not suit everyone, I know that it wouldn't be right for me or most women for that matter.'

'I'm so glad that you think that, but if I do talk about it, you won't tell Clive, will you? He doesn't hold with weakness and what he calls the counselling and blame culture.'

'No, of course, I won't.'

'Why don't we go into the summerhouse

out there? It's such a nice day and should be warm enough in the sun and out of the wind?'

'Good idea.'

'Sophie was five when I married Clive,' the woman said when they were sitting on the wicker chairs. 'He wasn't her father, you see, but you wouldn't have known it, he was absolutely devoted to her and so good with her, too. I only wish that she had taken to him as well, but she never did. I suppose it had a lot to do with the fact that I had a very hard time before I married Clive. I was thrown out of the house by my father and we lived in a tiny flat with a girl from work, who also had a baby. As a result, Sophie had never experienced close contact with a man before I married Clive. He couldn't have done more to win her over, but it didn't work and she went backwards and started to wet the bed and kept waking at night. A lot of men would have given up on her, but Clive didn't; he used to take her swimming — it wasn't something I had ever been able to do — and when she showed an aptitude for it, he paid for her to have one-to-one lessons. It was really for her that he had the swimming pool constructed, although he does like to use it himself. We went on holidays to the most wonderful places and he tried to help her with her homework, but it was no good and, believe me, the fault wasn't on his side. It's not every successful businessman who would only go to conferences during the school holidays, so that he could take his wife and daughter with him. He never went off on his own like a lot of people in his position do and he even took Sophie up to London sometimes and arranged for someone on his staff to take her to things like the London Eye and the museums in South Kensington.'

'Did Sophie's natural father have much to do with her?'

'No, he never saw her and didn't even know that I was pregnant when he left.'

'What about friends of her own age?' Fiona asked quickly, deliberately not looking in the woman's direction.

'You may find this difficult to believe, but I don't really know. She must have met lots of other girls at school and when she went riding, but she never invited anyone here, even though I told her any number of times that they would be welcome. She often used to go out on her bicycle and when I asked her where, she would always say something like: 'Oh, just for a ride.''

'Did she have any boyfriends?'

'That was the least of my worries — she was very young for her age.'

'What did you do about sex education?'

'I tried to introduce the subject, but she cut me short saying, 'we get all that stuff at school.' I suppose I ought to have persisted seeing how ignorant I was when I was a teenager, but I didn't — you see, I've never been comfortable talking about that sort of thing.' The woman shook her head. 'In fact, by that time I found it almost impossible to talk to her about anything. She used to spend hours alone in her room reading and it got so bad that I even suggested to Clive that we got a psychiatrist to see her, but he doesn't have any time for them; he thinks they do more harm than good and if one gets labelled as a psychiatric case, one is marked for life ... Finally, he thought that a change of school might be good for her, one where she would be able to take part in all the activities with boys and girls of her own age. A bonus was the lovely pool at Sandford College, which he had financed, and being on the board, he naturally carried a lot of influence and knew he would be able to get her in there.'

'How did she get on?'

The woman shook her head. 'I asked her to ring whenever she felt like a chat, but she never did. What did I do wrong?' She dabbed her eyes. 'Soon after we moved to this house,

I took a course in word processing and the use of the internet and did voluntary work for a cancer charity and so I wasn't so ignorant that I didn't worry that she might be on drugs. Clive is not the sort of person to invite confidences and I never told him about my fears and I even went to the length of searching Sophie's bedroom and bathroom, but although I looked everywhere, I found nothing. I also tried to see if there was anything about it on her computer, but there was a password on it and I wasn't able to access it.

'She never ate much and was very slight and another of my worries was that she might be developing anorexia, but there wasn't any real evidence of that, either, and evidently she always ate a reasonable lunch at her previous school. The really sad thing for me was she got much closer to her cat, Sammy, than she ever had been to Clive or me. I'll just get the photo album and show you what I mean.'

The woman got up and went back through the pool complex, coming back almost at once, sitting down and flicking through the pages until she found what she was looking for and then handed it across.

Fiona could see exactly what she had meant. The girl was looking down at the sleek black cat on her lap, one hand supporting the animal's head and there was an extraordinary expression on her face, a mixture of tenderness and sadness.

'Sophie never knew that I took that picture. I just happened to see her there as I was fetching Clive's camera for him. It was pure luck that it came out so well; I just looked through the viewfinder and pressed the button. It had one of those long focal length lenses and as I was quite a way away from her, she never heard the click. When I saw her expression using a magnifying glass, I had it enlarged and this is the result.' There was a long pause and then suddenly Celia looked up. 'Do you think that Sophie might have taken her own life?'

'It's impossible to rule it out at this stage. There's no doubt that she had taken a mixture of drugs, but that doesn't necessarily mean that she intended to kill herself. She might have had a fatal reaction to them, it happens from time to time.'

'Yes, I've read about that. I know it sounds ridiculous, but if that were the case, it would somehow make it at least a little bit better.'

'I don't think that's ridiculous at all, I know I'd feel exactly the same if I were in your position.'

The woman gave her a wan smile and then, as she looked over Fiona's shoulder, she slowly closed the album and got up.

'There are Clive and the Inspector. Shall we join them?'

'What a really lovely garden you have,' Fiona said when the two men came near. 'It's so peaceful and beautifully kept.'

'Yes, thanks to Celia and Luigi,' Hammond replied. 'I feel quite guilty about the fact that they do all the hard work and I just enjoy the fruits of their labours. We did worry that the extension with the pool might detract from it, but I don't think it does and with all the doors open, one gets the best of all worlds and is able to use the pool in the winter as well, with the doors closed.' He gave his wife a warm smile. 'Inspector Sinclair would like to take Sophie's computer, mobile phone and cassette recorder away for examination. I imagine that would be all right with you, my dear.'

'Yes, of course.'

'The Inspector's technical assistant hasn't quite finished upstairs. Why don't you have a cup of tea by the pool and I'll get Maria to take him one up there? If you'll excuse me, though, I have some work to do.'

Sinclair smiled. 'That's very kind of you, but we couldn't possibly impose on your hospitality any longer and Harris may be some time yet. Why don't we go for a walk in

Claremont Gardens and Harris can ring me on my mobile when he's finished and I'll pick him up?'

Hammond nodded. 'I take it you'll keep us informed of any developments.'

'Of course.'

Sinclair looked across at Fiona as they turned into the main road in the direction of Cobham. 'Don't worry, I'm not going to deprive you of some well-deserved refreshment; Claremont is a National Trust property and they have some excellent cakes in their tea shop and the park is lovely — one of Capability Brown's many efforts. Do you know about him?'

'Only by name.'

'He was lumbered with the first name of Lancelot. He laid out many eighteenth-century gardens, including Kew and Blenheim; lakes were a particular feature of quite a few of them. The one here is particularly beautiful.'

After their tea, they sat looking across the water and Fiona told him about her conversation with Celia Hammond.

'I don't think the poor woman's able to take in what's happened to her and I think she's dying to have a really long talk about it. I got the impression that her husband is very much one of those public school, stiff-upper-lip types; although they seem devoted to one another, I think that emotion and heart to hearts are completely alien to him, well mannered and pleasant though he seems to be.'

'Yes, I believe you're right. Bert might have been the man come to fix the television for all the interest he took in what he was doing. He just said: 'I'll leave you to it. I'm sure you won't want me hanging around getting in the way. Just knock on my study door if you want anything.' '

'Why do you suppose Clive Hammond married her? Celia is a pleasant-looking, obviously nice woman, but she clearly has a working-class background and was an unmarried mother, while, as you said, we know he's public school and with pots of money.'

'I don't know. It's not fair to label someone on a brief first meeting, but I can't see her being a ball of fire in bed, either. Although Hammond's very controlled, he's obviously a very driven and high libido sort of person and, if I'm right, I'd be very surprised if he doesn't enjoy that particular outlet elsewhere. As to his reasons for marrying her, quite a few highly successful men with that type of personality don't want competition at home. They find it comforting to have someone there who is both undemanding and thinks they're wonderful. Maybe he played the Professor Higgins with her when they were first married and perhaps he neither wanted nor needed a glamorous and socially accomplished wife to entertain his business contacts.'

Fiona nodded. 'What's next?'

'I've got to see Watson tomorrow and I'd like you to have a look at Sophie's riding school and speak to her house captain at the college and also the water polo fellow. Perhaps you'd give me a ring at my flat between nine and ten tomorrow evening. If, by any chance I'm not there, try my mobile.'

6

Vickie Dalton was on the phone when she heard the only just audible knock. 'Excuse me a moment, someone at the door.' She put her hand over the receiver and in response to her loud 'Come in' a young woman poked her head around the door and Vickie made a gesture towards the chair in front of her desk. 'Sorry about that,' she said when she had dealt with the caller. 'What can I do for you?'

'I'm DC Campbell and I'm making enquiries about a schoolgirl by the name of Sophie Hammond. I gather that she used to come here regularly.'

The woman pushed her warrant card across the desk and Vickie Dalton picked it up, looked at it carefully and then handed it back.

'Yes, she did. You said 'used', has she had an accident or something?'

'I'm sorry to have to tell you that she was found dead in bed recently at her new school.'

'Oh my God, that's awful!'

'How well did you know her?'

'Hardly at all. She used to ring to book a

ride and the only times I met her were when she arrived and then paid at the end. She was very shy and quietly spoken, but always extremely polite.'

'How did she pay?'

'In cash.'

'Did she go out alone?'

'No, it's one of my rules that apart from a few exceptions for people I know really well, riders must always be accompanied and she always asked for Tim, so much so, in fact, that she wouldn't come unless he was available.'

'Tim?'

'He's been with us for just over a year, having come straight from school. He's rather like Sophie in some ways, diffident and self-effacing; they obviously hit it off straight away. He desperately wants to be an event rider and, although he's talented and has an empathy with horses, particularly over the jumps, I don't think he's going to make it. He's not a risk-taker and an excess of caution never gets one anywhere in that particular game.'

'Why do you suppose that she only ever wanted to go with him? Do you think they were an item?'

'Good heavens, no. You've only got to talk to Tim for a couple of minutes to realise that he's scared stiff of girls. That's why he got on so well with Sophie — she clearly didn't threaten him in any way and from her point of view, I think she was so shy and withdrawn that having found someone with whom she was comfortable, she didn't want to risk anyone else. It was obvious to me that the rest of the staff here, all girls as it happens, were altogether too bouncy and extrovert for someone like Sophie.'

'You said threaten.'

'Poor old Tim! You should see one or two of the women who come here — talk about predatory females. You may know the type, too much money, not enough to do, with stressed and driven husbands and panting for a roll in the hay with a nice-looking young fellow, particularly after they've been sitting astride a horse for an hour. Tim's terrified of them and he makes me feel quite motherly.'

The policewoman didn't actually express her disapproval of such levity either by saying anything or by any overt change in her facial expression, but she still managed to convey it and Vickie Dalton had the strong feeling that the young woman would never have experienced such impulses herself. In fact, her body language was curiously redolent of the girl about whom she was enquiring.

'Who owns this school?'

'I do.'

Vickie Dalton deliberately said it aggressively, having decided that it would do the woman on the other side of the desk no harm at all to have her tail twisted a bit and she was gratified to see the flush spreading over her face.

'I'm sorry, I hadn't realised. The reason I asked was because I would like to have a word with the young man you mentioned and thought it would be tactful to ask the owner.'

Vickie could see at once that it would be only too easy to make the woman dig an even deeper pit for herself, but decided to let her off the hook.

'Yes, of course, I'll go and fetch him. You can use the staff rest room, if you like, you won't be disturbed at this time of day.'

Tim Harvey thought he was going to faint when the policewoman told him that Sophie had been found dead at her new school. He felt nauseous and light-headed.

'I'm sorry to have had to put it so directly, but I'm afraid there's just no way of breaking bad news like this gently. Did she seem low when you last saw her?'

'Do you mean that she killed herself?'

'We're still trying to discover exactly what happened.'

He never knew how he managed to get

through that interview. The policewoman had spoken quietly and hadn't threatened him or anything, but that didn't hide the fact that she was implying he might have been having sex with Sophie. The very idea was an insult to him and to Sophie; there had never been anything like that between them. He kept his answers as short and as non-committal as possible; yes, they had gone riding together quite often; no, she never said much at all, let alone about her personal life; no, they had never once seen each other away from the riding school; no, he most certainly didn't fancy her in the way she was implying; yes, she was always polite and pleasant, but never any more than that; yes, she was a competent rider; no, he knew nothing at all about her background; no, it wasn't unusual for him not to chat to the people he took out riding; if she didn't believe him, why didn't she ask Vickie?

'When did you last see Sophie?'

'We went for a ride the day before she was due to go to her new school. I can't remember the exact date, but Vickie would be able to tell you — it'll be in the appointments' book.'

'Did she seem her usual self?' Tim nodded. 'She didn't seem depressed or worried about anything?'

'No.'

When at last the woman had gone, he sat on a bale of straw near the stables, his head in his hands with tears rolling down his cheeks. When he was able to think straight again, he relived what had happened on his last ride with the girl.

They had been walking their horses slowly along a narrow path through the wood a couple of miles from the riding school and she was leading, when she suddenly reined in her mount and jumped down.

'Anything wrong?' he had asked, dismounting himself.

'I won't be able to come again until the Christmas holidays because I'm going to a new boarding school. I'm not very good at saying thank you, but I'd just like you to know how much I've enjoyed riding with you and you've been so nice to me. I didn't want to leave it until we got back to the stables, because if I did, I knew I might . . . '

To his dismay, he saw the tears rolling down her cheeks and felt his instinct taking over; he put his arms round her and hugged her until the choking sobs had stopped.

'It's all right,' he said, 'I won't tell anybody, I promise. Is there anything I can do to help?'

She took a step back and covered her face with her hands for a few moments and then took a handkerchief out of the pocket of her breeches and wiped the tears away.

'It's sweet of you to ask, but no one can help me, no one at all.'

She remounted and cantered off down the track at the end of the path with him following her and back at the school, jumped off and led her horse straight into its stable.

'I'm so sorry, Tim,' she said, when he followed her in on foot. 'I didn't mean to embarrass you — I don't know what came over me.'

He had thought that she was upset at having to move school and be leaving home for the first time. He knew that girls could get upset and emotional at certain times, but to think that she had killed herself . . .

★   ★   ★

Before driving back to Sandford College, Fiona decided that it would be stupid not to pay a visit to Sophie's old school, which was quite close to the riding school. It proved to be singularly unrewarding. The girl's form mistress had very little to add to what Fiona knew about her already. Yes, she was very quiet and well behaved, a lot brighter than the average and if anything she was over conscientious; no, she was not popular with the other girls. Why not? It was because she rebuffed attempts at friendship, failing to respond to any overtures in that vein and very soon such attempts were given up. No, she wasn't bullied and no, there were no hints that she might be taking drugs or having problems with boys.

On the drive back to Sandford College, Fiona was only too well aware both that she had gained almost nothing from the visits and that she had handled the young man at the riding school badly, not to mention Vickie Dalton. Sinclair would have assumed that the woman was the owner and if he had been wrong, she would have been flattered, whereas she had clearly managed to get off on the wrong foot with her right from the outset. What about Tim Harvey, though? He was hiding something, she was quite sure about that, but what? Had he been having sex with Sophie and was he also involved in drug taking? She had to admit that he didn't seem to be the type, but why else should he have been so uptight and nervous?

If she had been dissatisfied with the way she had managed Tim Harvey, her interview with Charlotte Winslow, the captain of Sophie's house did nothing to restore her confidence. The girl, as Margaret Rainsford had indicated, was brisk and confident.

'What's it like being House Captain?'

Fiona asked after she had introduced herself.

'It's great. I enjoy the responsibility.'

'Do you have any authority outside your house?'

'Oh yes, Henrietta, who is captain of the other girls' house, and I are on a par with the male college prefects. There are eight of us altogether, one of whom is Head, and Mr Manners has made it quite clear that, in future, if one of the girls should be the best candidate, he would have no hesitation in appointing her to that position.'

'Do the boys resent that situation?'

'You get the odd one, but it's not something I haven't been able to deal with.'

Fiona could believe it; the girl clearly wasn't in the least daunted by being interviewed by a police officer and very much doubted if she would be by anything else either.

'How well did you get to know Sophie Hammond?'

'As I told the headmaster recently, there were bound to be difficulties with some of the girls until they started to come here at the age of thirteen, like the boys. The problem is that by the time they get here at fifteen or sixteen, many of them find it very difficult to adapt. They're the ones who've either got regular boyfriends, have never been to a boarding school before, or, like Sophie, are totally unsuited to an environment like this.'

'In what way was she unsuited?'

'To get on well in a place like this you've got to fit in. It doesn't matter if you're not particularly good at school work or games, but you have to join in with things, be fun to have around and be enthusiastic. One of the most popular girls here is frankly not much good at anything except that she has the ability to take part in anything going both whole-heartedly and cheerfully. She's helpful and just makes people feel good. Sophie hardly joined in with anything. Out of class, she spent practically all her time either in her room working away at her project, or else at the pool and although I gather she was a really good swimmer, that didn't bring her into contact with others.

'The boys do have a water polo team, and no doubt, in time, with the new facilities, swimming will become a proper sport here, but it hasn't done so yet and she and the captain of the college water polo team were the only ones to practise outside the group swimming lessons that Miss Roberts has started.'

'I've met Miss Roberts, she's also house-mother, isn't she? How do you get on with her?'

'She's extremely efficient and straight forward. If she says she's going to do something, she does it right away. I like that.'

'She mentioned that one of the boys, Rob Preston, saw quite a lot of Sophie at the pool.'

'Yes, he's the water polo captain I just mentioned. I don't know him at all, only what he looks like, but it would surprise me if she had anything much to do with him. Sophie seemed afraid of her own shadow and I'd have thought she'd have run a mile if a boy took an interest in her. I knocked and went into her room one evening and she was washing at the basin. One soon gets pretty relaxed about being seen with nothing on in a place like this, but you should have seen her; she went into the most extraordinary contortions to hide herself with a towel. I apologised, of course, but pointed out that there was a bolt on the door and if she was that bothered it might be sensible to use it. I did make one more effort to chat to her, but it was like talking to a brick wall. Yes, she was settling in all right; no, there weren't any problems; no, she didn't have any questions; yes, she would be sure to ask if any cropped up. I suppose I ought to have tried harder, but there's only so much that one can do if one gets no response at all.'

'Have you heard any rumours about Sophie's death?'

'You mean about her taking an overdose?'

'Yes. I take it from your question that you have. How did they start?'

The girl raised her eyebrows slightly. 'People here are as quick on the uptake as most and your lot wouldn't be all over the place if she'd just had a heart attack or something like that, now would they?'

Fiona decided to let that one pass. 'Is there any sort of drug problem here?'

'According to my father, in his day it was a quick fag behind the bike sheds and six of the best if you were found out, now it's pot and instant expulsion for those using it. I don't know if anything like that's going on here now, but I wouldn't be surprised, it's been reported in the press enough times at other public schools. The same is probably true of alcohol.'

'What about sex?'

'I expect the odd girl and boy find a way, but there's never been an incident in the time I've been here. As for gay sex, some of the girls go in for cuddles and no doubt a bit more from time to time and one or two of the staff, male and female, are rumoured to be that way inclined, but despite the gossip, which I won't repeat, I doubt very much if they do anything about it. I must say that sex education is done very well here, at least for the girls — I don't know about the boys. Dr Peters doesn't believe in group talks — she told me it too often leads to sniggering and embarrassment. She carries out a medical exam on all the new girls and then has a talk to each of them. I remember that she said to me: 'you may ask me anything you like, anything at all, however ignorant you may think it makes you look or however embarrassed you may be about it. I will make no notes and everything you say will be entirely confidential. Remember, too, that this isn't your only chance; I'll give you my mobile phone number and if ever you want any advice I'll be only too pleased to come over.''

'Do any of the girls ever refuse the examination?'

'I shouldn't think so; people don't refuse to carry out reasonable instructions here and anyway, you'll have to ask Dr Peters about that.'

* * *

Rob Preston was swimming steadily in a slow crawl from end to end of the pool; his legs only moving sufficiently to keep his body balanced and horizontal. His mind, though, wasn't on his training, but on the girl who would no longer be able to join him. Up to that dreadful day he had worshipped Sophie. She was shy, like him, but she was so pretty and had such grace and skill in the water. She swam like a dolphin with seemingly no effort and yet for all his strength and effort, he wasn't anything like as quick as she was. They had got on so well and even though she didn't say much, she didn't need to when she had such a lovely smile and her quietness saved him from having to make conversation. Desperately shy himself, he had recognised the same in her immediately, which for him was one of her attractions. The one subject they were able to talk about easily was that of the great swimmers of the day and when he told her that if she got a good coach and worked hard she could easily become an international, she had blushed and said: 'Do you really think so?' She had seemed so pleased and excited that he had longed to give her a kiss, but he wasn't going to frighten her and if he took it gently, he just knew that their relationship would gradually develop.

Even Miss Roberts had been impressed by her. The woman was always criticising him, but never Sophie; how could she when, good though she was herself, she couldn't match the girl for speed. Even her superior strength was never able to compete with the elegance and smoothness of Sophie's timing. The butterfly was the only stroke she was able to do better, but then Sophie was only just learning the technique.

His world fell apart, though, one day Miss Roberts told him that she had to cancel the usual late afternoon swimming practice as Sophie had to catch up with work on her project. He had got so used to his regular workout in the pool that although he realised the complex might be locked, he decided to check to see if he could put in some time on his tumble turns — Miss Roberts might even be impressed.

The place was open and at first everything seemed to be in darkness, then he saw a faint gleam of light coming from the circular window in the door of the room, which Miss Roberts used as an office and which also doubled as a medical room for the doctor's visits. He was just about to knock when he saw that there was a gap in the curtains, which had been pulled across on the inside, and he looked through it.

Sophie was lying face down on the couch, with a towel draped across the middle of her body and, as he watched, Miss Roberts poured some oil on to the base of her neck and began to knead her shoulders with regular movements of her strong fingers. He knew that he shouldn't be spying on them, but he just wasn't able to drag his eyes away. At first, he could see that the girl's muscles were tight, the sinews standing out in her neck, but gradually she began to relax.

What he saw next sent a constricting pain like a band around his chest such that he was hardly able to breathe, surely Miss Roberts wasn't going to . . . The woman took hold of the end of the towel and slowly drew it down and then off altogether. Sophie's eyes opened wide and her head came back, but when the woman bent down and said something close to her ear, she slowly began to relax again.

Rob Preston had never seen any girl, let alone one of Sophie's age naked before and although it was only her back view, he couldn't believe how beautiful she looked. Her skin was so smooth and unblemished, the curve of her firm bottom so . . . he tried to drag himself away from that window, he really did, but when the woman began to massage her there, he just couldn't. He saw Sophie relax even more, when the hands moved down to her calves and then up to her thighs and once again higher still. This time the probing finger began to slide along the divide and when it delved deeper, Sophie gave a violent jerk, her head came right back and he saw the 'O' of her open mouth. He felt himself losing control and then he could hold it no longer, bent double he ran out, tears streaming down his cheeks.

His initial reaction had been a mixture of rage, disgust and betrayal, but that gradually changed to hatred of the woman responsible for what had happened to Sophie. The girl was obviously young for her age and totally inexperienced and how easy it would have been for Jo Roberts to get what she wanted. No doubt there had been other massages, which were not in the least threatening and it must have developed from there. The shame for Sophie must have been too much for her and was that the reason why she had killed herself? He couldn't think of a better one and that woman didn't deserve to get away with it. More than that, if he were half a man he would . . .

He had just reached the end of the length and was about to start his tumble turn when he became aware of the young woman standing at the end of the pool watching him.

'Hello,' she said, 'I'm Detective Constable Campbell. May I have a word with you about Sophie Hammond?'

He pulled himself up and then, acutely conscious of how brief his trunks were and even more of what had happened to him when he was thinking about Sophie and Miss Roberts while he was swimming and how the evidence was still there, flushed and turned away.

'I'll have a quick shower first and then change.'

'All right, I'll wait for you here.'

Preston glanced round at her as he went towards the changing room. Had she noticed? What was the matter with him? It had been happening with distressing regularity since, since . . . It wasn't even as if he thought the young detective that attractive. Indeed he hadn't been able to see all that much of her, hidden as she was by her felt hat and topcoat with its high turned-up collar.

'Is there anywhere else we might go?' she said when he got back. 'It's very stuffy in here.'

She had taken her hat and coat off and he could now see that she was slight and slim, looked tired and was not in the least threatening.

'The gym is just through there and there won't be anyone there at this time of day.'

As they sat down on one of the benches, he avoided looking at her and felt the pulse beating almost painfully in his neck.

'How well did you know Sophie?'

'Hardly at all. We just used to have special swimming coaching with Miss Roberts together — we weren't in the same form or anything.'

'How did you get on with Miss Roberts?'

Rob Preston looked down at the ground. Should he tell her, or not? It took him only a few moments to decide; if he did, it would only create endless trouble for himself and he knew how easily things like that got about. It would only be a short step for someone to start suggesting that he and Sophie had been . . . He suddenly became aware of the long pause and raised his head.

'I'm sorry, I've been very upset by what's happened and . . . '

'I asked how you got on with Miss Roberts.'

'She's all right; she's a very good coach and absolutely brilliant on the trampoline and springboard. She can do all the really difficult stuff such as somersaults and twists and her entries are always brilliant. She's always a bit tough on me — she's for ever saying that I don't work hard enough, which isn't fair, because I put everything I've got into it. She wasn't the same with Sophie, though, she was always nice to her.'

'In what way?'

Oh God, he thought, what have I let myself

in for now, and tried desperately to think of some way of putting it without letting the cat out of the bag.

'Well, praising and encouraging her and making suggestions about how she could continue to improve and getting her to practise her other strokes so that she could consider becoming a medley swimmer. Sophie found the butterfly difficult and that is something that Miss Roberts is good at, having such strong arms.'

'Did she do the same for you?'

'No, she said that I ought to concentrate on water polo, because I hadn't got the timing to excel at pure swimming.'

'Did you resent that?'

'No, why should I? She's quite right and she did show me how to work out with weights in the gym to develop my upper body strength.'

'Did it strike you that Sophie was at all depressed?'

'She was a quiet person and very shy and then so am I and that's why we got on well together.'

'Did you ever go to her room?'

'We aren't allowed to go into the girls' house at all.'

'Did you have sex together?'

Rob Preston's head jerked round and there

was a sudden constricting feeling right round his chest.

'How could you suggest such a thing? I'm not like that and if you must know, I haven't had sex with anyone.'

'What about Sophie?'

'Look, she and I just used to swim together, nothing more than that and I don't see why you have to make nasty insinuations.'

'I'm sorry, but some things were found in her room.'

'What sort of things?'

'Condoms.'

'I don't believe it — it just can't be true.' Rob Preston got to his feet.

'Don't go.'

'I'm not going to speak to you again unless my house-master's present as well.'

He had never been so angry or worried in all his life and stalked out without looking back. Even though he had been so upset and disillusioned by what he had seen only the week before, he now knew that the right thing would be to say nothing about it to anyone, let alone the police. He had read about the way they could twist even the simplest remark and now he had experienced it at first hand.

★ ★ ★

Fiona made her way slowly back to the car and sat there for several minutes before driving off. She was only too well aware that she had handled both Tim Harvey and Rob Preston badly. It didn't lighten her mood to know perfectly well that her problem wasn't just with a couple of young boys, she wasn't any good with men, full stop. To think that just about the only man who had behaved naturally with her in the preceding few weeks had been Rawlings, of all people. He was prepared to challenge her, make jokes at her expense and yet he never seemed in the least bit threatening and always seemed pleased to see her. She was even becoming tongue tied with Sinclair. That was something she didn't want to think about and started the engine, spinning the wheels as she accelerated violently on the loose gravel of the drive.

That evening she was watching an old film on TV, trying to blot out the negative thoughts that kept intruding. She hadn't been following the plot carefully and when, on the screen, the telephone rang by the side of the couple in bed, she jerked upright in the sofa suddenly remembering that she was supposed to ring Sinclair. In a panic, she looked at the clock and saw that it was nearly 10.15. To her relief, knowing what a stickler for punctuality he was, he was his usual polite self when she got through and gave him an account of her day's work, making no reference to the lateness of her call.

'The results of the detailed examination of Sophie's computer aren't ready,' he said, 'there was nothing of any significance on her CDs or DVDs, just a few films, mostly tearjerkers like 'Titanic' and some recordings of show jumping and all of Ian Thorpe's events at the Sydney Olympics. As for the fingerprints, none of them in Sophie's room are on the national database, so there's no point in pursuing that particular line. We may, though, have struck oil with the mobile phone which was in her room at home; it's interesting that it should be there rather than at the school, but perhaps they're not allowed there — I'll have to check with Miss Rainsford. Anyway, there are only a handful of numbers on it, such as the riding school, her dentist and so on, none of which is of any great interest, but there was a London number, which I had traced and I think a visit tomorrow afternoon to the address I was given might reap dividends. You remember Bob Appleyard?'

Fiona nodded. How could she forget how she had so nearly been killed during the Linda Baines case and how she had met the detective inspector who had been at the police college in Hendon with Sinclair.

'Well, he's got a somewhat twisted sense of humour on occasions and I don't altogether trust what he was hinting at, but I rang the number myself yesterday afternoon and there's no doubt that he was being perfectly serious this time. We shall just have to see for ourselves tomorrow. The address is somewhere in Earls Court and so I thought we'd better stick to the train. Why don't we meet at the station here in good time to catch the 2.30?'

'I'll be there.'

'Right.'

Fiona was about to ask him what he had been hinting at, but he had already rung off.

7

'How did you get on yesterday?' Sinclair asked when they had settled into the compartment on the train.

'Not all that well, I'm afraid.' Fiona gave him an account of her interviews with the three people she had seen the previous day. 'I felt I had to drop hints that the two young men might have been having a sexual relationship with Sophie and even though I may not have put it as delicately as perhaps I should have done, both of them were distinctly uptight at the suggestion, denying it vehemently and young Preston even walking out on me.'

'Did you believe them?'

'Well, if Sophie had left that window open, I'm sure an active young man like Rob Preston, particularly when it's obvious that testosterone is playing havoc with him at the moment, would have been able to climb into her room — I had a look at the fire escape from the outside after I had seen him and the traverse between it and the window looked perfectly possible to me.'

'I agree with that — the trunk of that

wisteria on the wall is pretty solid and although there were no footprints or debris on the ground below when Bert checked, that doesn't mean all that much considering how dry it's been. Although the top part of the window opens, you no doubt remember that the gap isn't all that big before it hits the stop. What sort of build does this young Preston have?'

'I have to admit that he probably wouldn't have been able to squeeze through; he's got big shoulders and is not much under your height.'

'There's also the fact that the window was locked. I suppose it's just possible that the three people whom we know went in there, Miss Rainsford, Manners and Dr McKintosh, might have locked it before our men arrived, but it seems unlikely to me. I will check on that, though. Tell me more about the boy at that riding school?'

'He seemed frightened to death of me, but the woman who runs the place says he's always like that, particularly where females are concerned, and he certainly gave me the impression of being painfully shy and diffident. Nevertheless, I had the distinct impression that he was hiding something.'

Fiona had felt herself blushing when she first mentioned Preston, remembering what she had seen as he pulled himself out of the pool and trying to suppress the memory by forcing herself to think of something else, but that only made it worse. At least, though, Sinclair seemed not to have noticed, being at that moment deep in thought and staring out of the window. It happened again, though, when he turned towards her a little later on and explained what appeared to be going on at the address he had been given when he had rung the phone number the previous day, which had been found on Sophie's mobile phone.

The road was only a short walk from Earls Court underground station and there was a man hovering at the top of the stone steps leading to the basement of one of the tall houses which formed part of the long terrace.

'I would suggest that you try a different form of entertainment this afternoon,' Sinclair said softly.

The man swivelled round. He seemed about to reply but then changed his mind abruptly when he caught sight of the detective's warrant card. He then scuttled rapidly away.

There was an entryphone by the side of the door and when Sinclair pressed the button on it, there was a moment's pause and then a disembodied voice said: ''ello.'

'I rang earlier.'

There was a loud click, the door opened a crack and a plump, middle-aged woman came out of a door at the side of the lobby as he stepped inside.

'Come on in, dearie. She's a lovely girl, 36 22 36 and . . . '

She suddenly caught sight of Fiona and some of the colour went out of her cheeks.

'I'm sorry, luv, we don't do couples.'

'Police,' Sinclair said, showing his card again. 'We want to ask you about one of the girls who used to work here.'

'You'd better come in 'ere.'

The room contained a small sofa and two easy chairs, a table on which was an electric kettle, cups, milk and sugar on a tray and by its side, a telephone.

'I'd better take this orf the 'ook,' she said, laying the receiver down on its side.

'So you recognise her?' Sinclair said, when he saw the woman's expression as she looked at the photograph he was holding out.

'Yus. 'as anyfink 'appened to 'er?'

'Why do you ask?'

'She was 'ere several times the summer just gone when I were fillin' in for the woman who's usually 'ere who'd been taken ill like. I don't know whether that girl came back later. Certainly she didn't when I was 'ere. Called 'erself Vickie, she did and she was into the 'eavy stuff.'

'Did you know that she was only sixteen?'

'Wot! She told me she were eighteen and it's up to the woman who interviews 'em to check that sort of fing. Mind, she did look young and she were a strange girl.'

'Strange? In what way?'

'Well, she spoke proper and was always quiet and polite and yet she let the punters do all the heavy stuff.'

'What sort of heavy stuff?'

The woman glanced at Fiona and then turned back towards Sinclair. 'There's no pressure on the girls 'ere; they say wot they're prepared to do to the woman who selects 'em before they start — there is a minimum, of course — and then they're paid accordin'. Some, like Vickie, are prepared to do anal and although most are quite 'appy to dish CP aht, not many are prepared to receive it an' if they do it's allus very light.'

'And she was different?'

'Yeah. There is a panic button, but she never used it and she gave value orl right, I saw the results a few times. Naughty schoolgirl was one of her most popular tricks — we 'ave all the gear 'ere, see.'

'Why do you suppose she was willing to do that?'

'I 'ave come across a few girls who are into it and like it — it's usually the lessers — but I reckon Vickie was in it for quick money — it pays the best, yer see. She also said something funny once after one of the punters had really laid into 'er.'

'What was that?'

'She said that she'd done something real bad and deserved it.'

'Any idea what that something was?'

The woman shook her head. 'She didn't say and I've fahnd it best not to ask abaht that sort of fing.'

'How do the girls find a place like this?'

'That's not somefink I concern myself wiv.'

'Who runs this place?'

'I wouldn't tell yer, even if I knew, which, as it 'appens I don't. There is a woman who sees all the girls before they start and a different geezer comes to collect the money each evening and pays the maid and the girls. I'm not a regular 'ere now and they give me a bell when I'm wanted. I 'ave to say this for 'em, they always play it straight and we always do the same. There are stories about people tryin' to short change 'em and it ain't worth the risk.'

'How did you get into it yourself?'

'Mate of mine did it before me. She got ill — cancer it was — and she told me abaht it.

I used to do cleaning jobs, but I like it 'ere and it's not as if I do full time now, I fill in when any of the other women leave and they can't find an immediate replacement, or are off sick or taking a break. Most of the girls are nice enough and I like to 'ave a bit of company and so far, I've 'ad no trouble with the punters.'

'I'd like a word with the girl working here this afternoon if she's free.'

'You're welcome to, but it won't get you very far.'

'Why not?'

'She's from Eastern Europe and her English is about as good as my Polish. You needn't get excited, the woman who brought 'er 'ere showed me 'er passport and said she was legal.'

'How does she communicate with the clients?'

'She doesn't. The other woman told me what she was prepared to do and I negotiate the price an' that with the punters. It's turned out OK so far.'

'Does the Polish girl come every day?'

'Nothing regular like. Just a couple of times a week now.'

'Well, thanks for your help,' Sinclair said after they had seen the rather plump girl with dyed blonde hair, with whom it proved just as impossible to communicate with as the woman had suggested.

'Fink nothing of it. Is Vickie in bad trouble, then?'

'I'm afraid she's dead.'

The woman's hand went to her mouth. 'Poor little fing,' she said, wiping a tear away from her cheek.

'Don't move,' Sinclair said. 'We'll find our own way out.'

As the two detectives reached the front door, they heard the phone ringing.

'What did you make of her?' Sinclair asked as they made their way to the underground station.

'I thought she was rather nice — a motherly sort of woman.'

'Hmm. I need to have a serious think about this and I'm also going to have a chat with Appleyard this afternoon. As I'm busy tomorrow, why not have a break until after the weekend and I'll see you in the office on Monday at nine, all right?'

Fiona had been deeply upset by what she had heard in the flat and it wasn't all right at all. She desperately wanted to talk it over with someone and she knew that just at the moment Sinclair would not be the right person. But who else was there? The answer came to her on the way back on the train, but suppose he refused to see her? There was only one way to find out and so early the following morning, her heart beating painfully in her chest, she plucked up all her courage, drove to the hospital, walked up to the door in the pathology department and knocked loudly.

'Come in.'

'Do you think that Dr Rawlings would see me for a few minutes?'

Miss Ryle gave her a rather wintry smile.

'I doubt it. He normally never sees people without an appointment, but I can but ask.'

'Would you? That would be very kind.'

The woman was about to say that kindness didn't enter into it, knowing perfectly well that there would be an almighty explosion if Rawlings found out that she had sent the rather wan-looking woman away without consulting him, particularly as she seemed to have the knack of at least partially neutralising the man's acerbic persona. She wasn't entirely surprised, either, when the pathologist not only agreed to see her, but even seemed quite enthusiastic about the idea.

'Bring her in, Miss Ryle, we mustn't keep the young lady waiting, must we?'

Rawlings didn't get up when Fiona was shown in, he merely looked at her over the top of his half moon spectacles and gestured towards the chair in front of his desk.

'What can I do for you, my dear?'

She told him about the telephone number being found on Sophie's mobile phone and their subsequent visit to the basement flat in Earls Court.

'I can just about understand that a sixteen-year-old girl might decide to go into prostitution to finance a drug problem, but why should she submit herself to being beaten and perverted sex.'

'You mean the anal variety?' Fiona nodded. 'Well, in addition to male homosexuals, plenty of heterosexual couples like it as an occasional diversion and some even prefer it. It has a very long history, well back into classical times, and even today in the so-called primitive societies, it is even practised in place of a contraceptive.'

'What about prostitutes?'

'Some are prepared to take it on; there was a paper on it with reference to drug addicted prostitutes in Scotland even doing it without condoms, hence the high incidence of positive HIV in that group.'

'What I can't understand is how a sixteen-year-old girl like Sophie could have got herself into a situation like that. She had all the material advantages.'

'An affluent background doesn't protect young people from drugs, you know.

Hereditary factors may also play a part; do you know anything about her natural father? I gather that she was adopted.'

'Yes, she was, but her mother didn't say anything to me about him other than that he had never even seen the girl and I didn't feel I could pursue the matter any further as I'd only just met the woman for the first time. Sophie, though, was clearly a lot brighter than average and athletically gifted — the staff at both the schools she went to recently were quite clear about that — and that is not true of her mother. As soon as Celia Hammond's own father discovered that she was pregnant, he turned her out. She didn't say anything about being abused herself, but it wouldn't surprise me; she did tell me that he was a bully and her manner and body language when she said it strongly suggested to me that she'd been abused.'

'Now, the fact that the girl appears to have sought corporal punishment actively is an interesting one. When I first qualified,' Rawlings said, 'and hadn't much money, I used to supplement my income as a junior doctor by doing some evening and weekend work in a women's prison. I became interested in the phenomenon whereby quite a few of the girls cut themselves. I say girls advisedly because it was the younger age group who, by and large, were the ones to do it. I also discovered that other adolescent girls not in prison, some of them by no means disadvantaged, were in the habit of doing this. Most of them said the same thing, that it made them feel calmer and helped their feelings of intolerable tension and frustration. Why girls? Certainly in my experience, young men very seldom do it — they are much more likely to act aggressively and violently against others. What is the explanation for this sex difference, which is rather like that in anorexia nervosa and bulimia? Is it due to lack of self esteem engendered by centuries of male oppression, as feminists would have us believe, or is it hormonal or even due to other differences in brain chemistry? Your guess is as good as mine.

'Now, the case you describe is certainly unusual. The prostitution side, as you say, is understandable in drug addicts — in what other way are they able to get hold of money on that scale and quickly? Rent boys are often in the same situation. As for being beaten on the backside, many men go to prostitutes so it can be done to them probably because either wives or girl friends won't do it, or the men don't want them to know of their desires in that direction. Prostitutes aren't judgmental — they just do it. Many men also like the idea of beating women and girls — it has been a common theme of pornographers for centuries — and quite a few couples do it as a form of sex play, but usually only on special occasions. Interestingly it is reasonably common in lesbian couples and submissive females in that context seem to enjoy being on the receiving end. However, none of that seems to apply in the case of this girl, Sophie, and I can't say I have ever come across one as young as her actively encouraging corporal punishment, let alone saying that they were seeking it for having done something seriously wrong.'

'Was there any evidence that Sophie had had a recent beating?'

'No, there was no sign of recent bruising anywhere and no scarring, either, so she hadn't been cutting herself — the forearms are the most common site for that. On occasions I have come across masochistic behaviour as a consequence of physical abuse as a child and there is that hoary old idea that beatings at public schools in days gone by were quite often followed by a desire for that sort of thing in adulthood. I must say, though, that the evidence for that is pretty weak.'

'Why does sex have to be so sordid?'

'The answer to that one is quite clear: it

doesn't, but problems in that regard are very common. Despite what the feminists of this day and age say, many women don't enjoy it all that much and quite a few don't enjoy it at all. When I was doing clinical medicine, you wouldn't believe the number of times I heard women in the older age group say: 'my husband's very good, he doesn't bother me much!' I don't believe that the situation's all that different now; the big change has been that it is now the fashion for the pundits to maintain that women enjoy it more than men, when every reliable survey points in the opposite direction. What seems to be clear is that men can enjoy it with almost anyone, whereas in women there usually has to be emotional involvement as well, although just because that is true in broad statistical terms, it isn't always the case and the roles can be reversed. What often gets forgotten is that sex shouldn't be too reverential; there is a time for that, but it should be fun as well.' He paused, looking at her intently for a few moments. 'Is there anything else you wanted to ask?'

'Do you think there is any possibility that Sophie's death could have been accidental?'

'You mean that she might just have been taking recreational drink and drugs and have accidentally overcooked it?' Fiona nodded.

'No, but as to convincing the coroner and your senior colleagues, that is quite another matter.'

'Well, thank you very much, both for seeing me and for your patience. I've learned a lot.'

The man nodded. 'Feel free to come again should the need arise; I'm always happy to try to answer intelligent questions — on any subject. By the way, if you're not doing anything on Saturday I wonder if you'd like to come to lunch with us, my wife and me, that is.'

'I'd like that very much,' Fiona said, almost without thinking.

'Before you commit yourself totally I should warn you that there's a sting in the tail. Our rather rumbustious eight-year-old granddaughter, who quite literally never stops talking, has been dumped on us while riding out a distinctly unimpressive attack of varicella — that's chicken pox to the classically illiterate.' The man grinned at her. 'Not, of course, that you're one of that depressing brigade. Anyway, she's due back home on Sunday with school on Monday and I've rashly promised her a visit to our local theme park, or whatever one's supposed to call the bloody things, before she does so. My wife resolutely refuses to go near those whirligig things that Rebecca delights in and

154

in my old age, being vestibularly challenged, they provoke nausea and even worse in me. She's too young to go on them on her own and I don't suppose you would be game to do the honours, would you?'

'I don't see why not.'

'Capital! I shall sit at a safe distance and enjoy the spectacle. By the way, here's my card with our address and home number should you get cold feet. Should we say about twelve-thirty? By the way, don't dress up whatever you do — jeans and a jumper fit the bill admirably.'

On her way back to her flat, Fiona's initial reaction to the pathologist's invitation had been one of relief that she wouldn't have to occupy the whole weekend on her own, but then the doubts began to creep in. Suppose the man was playing some ghastly practical joke on her and, when she arrived, lunch turned out to be a formal affair with the local vicar in attendance and the man's wife dressed to the nines, pearls around her neck and a disdainful expression on her face as she looked the scruffy figure in jeans up and down? And what if the meal started with something like oysters? She had never even tried one, but just knew that she would never be able to get one down, the very thought of the slippery, salty things provoked a spasm of nausea.

Was it even possible that Rawlings's interest in her had a sinister aspect and that he had designs on her? Suppose he wasn't even married and she found herself alone with him? Why else should he have been so pleasant to her, when he treated his secretary in such a cavalier fashion?

Deeply ashamed of herself, she felt the tears welling up and forced herself to concentrate on the road ahead, but when she got back to her flat, it all became too much and she threw herself on to her bed and let herself go, pounding the pillow and sobbing and crying out loud until she was utterly exhausted.

★   ★   ★

The following morning, Fiona still had doubts and just before she was due to leave, her hand even hovered over the telephone on the bedside table, but with sudden determination, she turned away from it and strode out to her car parked in the road outside.

Her fears turned out to be groundless, Mrs Rawlings proving to be an ample, jolly woman, who got up from the kneeler, on which she had been doing some weeding, as

Fiona unlatched the front gate of the large detached house.

'Hello, m'dear, you must be Fiona; I'm Helen.' She pulled off her gardening glove and gave the detective a bone crunching handshake. 'I hope you're feelin' strong; one never knows what that dreadful man is goin' to let people in for. Picnic's in the car; nothin' fancy, but I expect you'll find somethin' you like. Rebecca'll only eat ham, hard-boiled eggs and an apple if she's bullied. Are you good at bullyin' small girls? I always tell her if she doesn't do what I say, I'll whack her with my hair brush. I don't mean it, of course, and I wouldn't mind bettin' that she knows it, too; it's a little game we play and she goes along with it. She's a nice little thing, really.'

At that moment, Rawlings appeared, holding hands with the girl, who was bouncing up and down beside him. Dressed in slacks, check shirt and jumper and sporting a bush hat, the man looked so different from his usual self that Fiona was hard pressed not to grin.

That set the tone for the whole afternoon. From the very start, as Rawlings had warned her, Rebecca chattered incessantly, hardly having time to draw breath. It started when

Fiona had considerable difficulty in shutting the front passenger door of the battered Volvo estate.

'Rebecca, you'll have to do your stuff.'

'OK, Gramps.'

The girl got out, pulled the door back as far as it would go and then, taking a run at it, slammed it shut as hard as she could. The whole vehicle rocked violently and with a cheeky grin, she jumped into the back.

'That's the ticket!'

The car lurched off in a series of jerks and straight away the voice piped up from behind.

'I call them Joey hops, 'cos they're too small for a kangaroo. Do you know what a Joey is, Fiona?'

'You tell me.'

She did, at great length and about wallabies and other marsupials as well. 'Why don't you get a new car, Gramps?' the girl asked, when she had covered the remaining fauna of Australia.

'Because I'm fond of the old girl. Think for a moment about that old Teddy of yours. He's a bit battered, but you wouldn't want to get rid of him, now would you?'

'I suppose not.'

'There's no supposing about it; of course, you wouldn't.'

'Gramps knows a lot about Teddies, you know, Fiona.'

'I'm sure he does.'

She was just about to say that he knew a lot about most things, but was saved from that embarrassment by the continuing flow from behind.

'I like the colour of your jumper, Fiona,' the girl said and from then on kept it up, hardly stopping to catch her breath until they arrived.

'What's your favourite ride?' Fiona asked as they got out.

'What I'd really like to do is go on Montezuma's Revenge; may I, please Gramps?'

'Only if Fiona's brave enough to go with you.'

'You will, won't you, Fiona? My friend told me it was really scary.'

'Lunch first and then we'll see,' her grandfather interjected. 'In any case, you'll have to start with something gentle otherwise you might really get it.'

'Get what, Gramps?'

'Montezuma's revenge, of course.'

'What's that, then?'

'I'll tell you when you're a bit older. Now, come along, let's watch the seals while we tackle the lunch basket that Mops has prepared.'

At least, Fiona thought, while they tucked into the picnic, it stemmed the flow. It was only too clear, too, that Mrs Rawlings had been exaggerating about the girl's food fads; Rebecca steadily munched her way through everything that Rawlings handed out. It was all both plentiful and delicious. There were chicken and ham sandwiches, pork pies, cold sausages, tomatoes, lettuce and cheese and Cox's apples. A bottle of hock had also been provided for them, while Rebecca made assaults on the tins of ginger beer.

'May I have an ice-cream, Gramps?'

'Only if you don't say a single word for the next fifteen minutes while we have our coffee. One single word and no ice-cream — understood?'

The girl opened her mouth to reply and then closed it again abruptly and nodded as he held up his hand.

'I'll let you know how you're doing every five minutes. Now go and sit over there and watch the seals with your drink so that Fiona and I can have a quiet chat.'

Rawlings grinned at Fiona as the child did as she had been told. 'The secret with her is always to carry out exactly what one says or threatens with absolutely no exceptions. Sugar with your coffee?' He laughed when she shook her head. 'So you weren't above joining in the Miss Ryle baiting? Don't worry, she loves it.'

With Rawlings bellowing out the time at each five minute interval, Rebecca managed to hold out. Once the promised ice-cream had been consumed, she took Fiona's hand and led her to the queue for the ghost train, once again chattering nonstop. To her utter astonishment, Fiona had more fun that afternoon than she had had for . . . No, she was wrong, she had never in her life ever had so much fun. There was the pleasure of sharing the excitement of the small girl as they went on ride after ride. She let herself go and screamed with the best of them as the roller-coaster plunged down and, sitting right at the front, they went down the water chute, their hair getting soaked and even braved Montezuma's Revenge, a fiendish device which rotated in a series of giant circles while the car in which they were secured spun on its own axis.

'I know,' Rebecca said as Fiona walked unsteadily away by her side, 'why don't we try the carousel now — that's nice and gentle?'

Rawlings watched as they went round and round at a stately pace, the horses moving slowly up and down. Fiona's hair was tousled, there was colour in her cheeks and she was even laughing at something Rebecca was saying.

'Time to go,' he said as they came towards him after the ride had finished, the small girl skipping along beside her.

'Must we, Gramps?'

''Fraid so, dear. Come along, I need you to do your stuff with the car door; we can't possibly have Fiona falling out on the way back, now can we?'

After less than five minutes, Rawlings glanced over his shoulder, while they were waiting in a short queue at a roundabout.

'Thank God! She's asleep and blessed silence is just what's needed, as I have a proposition to make to you. No, not that sort of proposition,' he said, his lips twitching as he glanced across and saw the expression on her face, 'one that I hope will interest you. You see, I have just managed to negotiate the funding for a specialist technician in my department — I have been making do with a part-timer, shared with clinical pathology. We haven't been able to keep up-to-date and I have had to send specimens away for the latest analysis techniques, which is both time consuming and unsatisfactory. If I send them to another NHS laboratory, I get a second-class service and if I use the private sector, it is prohibitively expensive.'

'Where do I come in?'

'I would like to offer you the job. You

would, of course have to be properly trained, but I feel sure you would take to it. You did well at school and your experience on the front line of criminal police work would prove invaluable. You also need have no worries about pay — I would be able to match your present level and, if you work hard, who knows, you might be able to get an open university degree and become a university lecturer in due course. That is, of course, a long way ahead, but why not be un-English about it. I am not an admirer of everything that our trans-Atlantic friends do, but their 'sky's the limit' attitude has much to commend it.'

'But I couldn't possibly give up my present job, not in the middle of a case like this and there's Inspector Sinclair to think about.'

'I wasn't proposing to ask you to do that and I think you'd find that Sinclair would be sympathetic. One of the advantages of having a reputation for being brutally direct is that people begin to expect it of one and I am going to indulge myself in some direct speaking now. You are in the wrong job, young Fiona, and I wouldn't mind betting that that is one of the reasons for your being so depressed. I feel free to say this because, you see, I know what I'm talking about; I did very well in my medical studies and got prizes and the pick of the house jobs at my teaching hospital, but it soon became only too clear both to my mentors and to me, that clinical medicine was not my forte.

'Flippancy and impatience with those who were either swinging the lead, or even lacking moral fibre, to use the terminology of that day, were not characteristics I could cover up in the long term, they were not going to go away and to say I lacked empathy with patients would have been an understatement. Medicine, though, has, of course, a very broad canvas and pathology, in particular the forensic variety, suited me down to the ground. I immediately enjoyed the intellectual challenge of it and the sparring with coroners and other members of the legal fraternity. There is a long tradition of forensic pathologists being acerbic — the very first one, Sir Bernard Spilsbury, was noted for it — and others seemed naturally to follow suit. I discovered that I was good under cross-examination, having the ability to get under the skin of most QCs and the same applied to some of the more pompous of my senior colleagues and not only was I good at it, I positively enjoyed it. I can't deny that a lot of it is a pose; one starts being acid-tongued and outspoken as part of the act and then it becomes a habit. There are some, like the admirable Miss Ryle, Sinclair and you, my dear, who have got my number and in your differing ways give as good as you get, but there are lots of others who don't, which makes it easier for me to stick to my opinions. There are dangers, of course, but I am lucky in having a wife who knows precisely when and how to do judicious balloon pricking when necessary.

'Why am I boring you with all this? It's because I'm concerned about you. It is quite clear to me that you have a real flair for detective work, but what you most certainly do not have a flair for is dealing with the sad and vicious people you come across and in particular the abused. One can either leave behind memories of abuse and sadness in the past, or let it blight one's life for good and become a perpetual victim. It is no easy matter to overcome, but one thing is very clear and that is that reinforcing traumatic memories daily in the course of one's work is just about the worst thing one can do. That is why I believe that a move would be very much in your interest.'

'Do you think that a person who has suffered sexual or physical abuse ever gets over it?'

'Most certainly. I had an uncle who was a prisoner of war of the Japanese and worked on the Siam railway. He was treated quite abominably, as indeed they all were, but when I knew him he was forward looking, cheerful as the day is long and lived a happy and productive life into his middle eighties. How did he do it? I suspect it was in large part due to his being born with the right personality. He had no truck with victimhood and the compensation culture. What about those who are more introspective and less able or even unable to put it behind them and who are haunted by their experience? One thing is certain and that is that they are deeply unhappy and will remain so unless they can come to terms with what has happened to them. There is a further difficulty if memories of the past are constantly being reinforced, which, I venture to suggest is what is happening to you at present, now that you are immersed in this very sad Sophie Hammond case. Well, there you are. Why not think about the idea? There's no hurry, no hurry at all.'

'There are bound to be other questions later, but I do have one now.'

'Fire away.'

'How did you find out about me?'

'I didn't. Put it down to the intuition of a man who isn't quite as insensitive to others as some people think.'

When they got back, to Fiona's relief, Rawlings seemed to sense that she needed to get away and after a hug from the still sleepy Rebecca and having thanked his wife for the picnic, she was shown out to her car and when she had got in and wound down the window, he bent down.

'You made a palpable hit with young Rebecca,' he said. 'While you were saying goodbye to Helen, she asked me if you could come again when she was next staying with us. I'm really most grateful; entirely thanks to you, her last day went with a real swing.'

'I had a really lovely time myself, really lovely — I don't know how to thank you. I . . .'

He saw the tear forming at the corner of her eye and banged loudly on the side of the door.

'Drive carefully,' he boomed and strode back towards the house.

8

Although he hadn't shared his doubts with Fiona, Sinclair was deeply uneasy about the flat in Earls Court and he said as much to Bob Appleyard when he went up to London again the following day and saw his friend at the Yard.

'I don't know the first thing about places like that and it's difficult to put my finger on it, but that 'maid' was just a little too pat in what she said and her accent slipped a bit from time to time. There's no doubt that sex for sale was going on there all right — there was a bloke about to go in when we arrived — but if the girls are vetted as carefully as the woman suggested, why was Sophie Hammond allowed to work there when by all accounts she didn't even look her sixteen years. What I really need to do is talk to one of the girls, one, that is, who can speak English.'

'You most certainly shouldn't do that on your own. These days, you have to watch out for investigative journalists like a hawk. The tabloids have sources which make ours look like those of the Bow Street Runners and it's just not worth taking that sort of risk. Where's your sidekick?'

'That's one of the reasons I've come to see you. She's still more than a bit fragile following that Baines case: she should have taken a long break, which I suggested, but she refused to do so and, more than that, I'm not even sure she's up to this type of work at all; she identifies with victims, real and imagined far too much.'

'Hmm, I see the problem. I tell you what, why don't I have a word with my Super and he might know of someone suitable who would be able to give you a hand for an hour or two.'

Sinclair pursed his lips. 'Thanks for the offer, but I'm not sure that I ought even to have spoken to you about it. It would do me a power of no good if my Super, a bloke called Watson, were to hear about me even thinking of going over his head. He long ago made his views only too clear about those of us who have a university background and he's only put me in charge of this case because it involves a private boarding school and he also wants to keep the Chief Constable, who's on the board, sweet.'

'Tyrrell here is not like that at all.'

In the event Sinclair was to think later, it could hardly have gone better. Tyrrell proved to be friendly, no doubt, he thought, helped by the fact that they had both been to Oxford and were golfers, and he clearly saw no reason why Watson's permission should be sought.

'I'm sure that Sergeant Prescott would be only too pleased to have a chat with you about it,' he said. 'For some time now she's been heavily involved in the pursuit of a prostitution ring which has been bringing in girls from eastern Europe and what she doesn't know about those on the game in London isn't worth knowing. She's catching up with paperwork today and I'm sure she'd help you out for a couple of hours. I'll give her a ring right away.'

Mark Sinclair took an immediate liking to the young woman; she was both cheerful and outgoing and the contrast to Fiona Campbell, who was both tense and obviously unhappy, could hardly have been more striking.

'I'd very much value your comments,' he said after he had described the case he was working on and his reservations about the 'maid' in the flat in Earls Court.

The young woman thought for a moment. 'In my experience, the people running places like the one you described would never risk taking on an anyone underage and from what you said that girl Sophie encouraged her clients to beat her for real — that's something I've never come across. Some girls are quite happy to lay it on and even accept a light spanking, but not the real thing. On top of that, you also said that Sophie didn't look or behave like someone of eighteen. Would you mind if I made a suggestion?'

'No, of course not.'

'I'm intrigued by that place you described; I don't understand why they agreed to take Sophie on and I'd like to see it for myself, with you of course.'

'Are you sure you can spare the time?'

'I'd better clear it with Tyrrell, but I can't see him objecting.'

★   ★   ★

The woman who answered their ring at the flat in Earls Court was the same one Sinclair had seen the day before and was it his imagination, he wondered, or was she nervous in a way she hadn't been on the previous day?

'As I'm sure you realised,' Sinclair said when he had introduced Sarah Prescott, 'the Polish girl wasn't able to help me yesterday because of the language difficulty and I'd like to have a word with the woman working here today.'

'She's got a client with her at the moment and there's another one waiting.'

'Then he'll have to wait a bit longer, won't he? How does she let you know when she's free?'

'She comes in here and then when the punter leaves she goes for a wash.'

'What's the problem then?' Sarah said. 'We'll wait here and when she appears, you can get rid of the satisfied customer and clean up.'

'What about the other bloke?'

'I'm not running this place, you are. Give him a mag or show him a video and don't tell me you haven't got any.'

At that moment, a tall, blonde young woman, wearing a white towelling dressing gown and slippers came in.

'Police,' Sinclair said, when the other woman had left, 'sorry to interrupt your work, but as I explained to the other lady, the girl in this photo was found dead recently and the number of this place was found on her mobile. I was wondering if by any chance you recognise her.'

The young woman tried but failed to hide the fact that she found Sinclair's manner and approach hilariously funny.

'Don't get me wrong, I'm really sorry to hear about the girl, but where I come from, the police aren't anything like you.'

'Bondi beach?'

She grinned at him. 'Not a million miles from there. No, I can't help, I'm afraid. I've only been here for four weeks or so and she hasn't been here during that time. Apart from that, I don't ever meet the other girls.'

'How much longer are you planning to go on working here?'

'I've decided to move on at the end of next week.'

'Any questions, Sarah?'

'Yes. Why are you working in a place like this?'

'Because the pay's good, the hours are reasonable and I enjoy it. I need money to finance the next stage of my world trip and I'm nearly there.'

'You enjoy it?'

The young woman smiled. 'Almost all the blokes are really nice and that's not all — they're clean, polite and grateful and are prepared to accept no for an answer, which is more than you can say about the people you meet in other sorts of job in London, or so my mates tell me. Perhaps you wonder if I ever come? Sometimes, if I feel like it and the bloke happens to press the right buttons, and I'm quite happy to fake it if they want a command performance — you know, 'Sally meeting Harry' sort of stuff.'

'That sounds a bit too good to be true to me.'

'That's just what I thought when a girl I know from back home told me she was leaving and that they'd always treated her right and that I ought to give it a go. I gave the place a once over, some woman asked me a few questions, had a look at me in the altogether and gave me an address to go to for an AIDS test and a check up — I'm sure you know the sort of check up I'm referring to. I was quite impressed. As I said, I've no complaints so far. Mind you, it's not something I'd want to do for too long, but then you could say that about a lot of jobs, couldn't you?'

'What sort of things do you have to do?'

'You sound interested.'

Sarah wasn't in the least put out. 'I wouldn't make much of a fist of my present job if I wasn't, now would I? Perhaps, though, the use of the word fist isn't entirely appropriate.'

The young woman gave her a broad grin. 'Good on you. I was going to say that the bottom line is that I don't 'have' to do anything, only things that are acceptable to me, but that might be misunderstood. And what are they? Straight sex, French, hand jobs

174

and handing out cp and I'm prepared to dress up a bit, schoolgirl, air hostess, nun — we've got quite a bit of gear.'

'What sort of cp?'

'Hand spanking, slipper, tawse or cane, but no whips or riding crops and no blood.' She gave another grin. 'The ones who like it hard appreciate my wrist action, that's thanks to having played a lot of squash.'

'Do you ever let them do it to you? We've been told that the girl whose photo we showed you appears to have wanted to be beaten really hard.'

'No way!'

'There is evidence,' Sinclair said, 'that the girl in the photo had had anal sex if not regularly, at least fairly often. Are many of the girls prepared to do that?'

'I'm not the person to ask. I certainly won't, but I have heard that it's done by some of them.'

'Here?'

'The woman who interviewed me asked me if I was prepared to do it, but accepted my saying no without pressing me in any way.'

'What sort of woman was she?'

'Nothing like the 'maid' here you've just met. She was smartly dressed, didn't speak down to me, rather like you, if I may put it that way and she was business-like as well;

she wanted to see my ID, was quite straight forward in her questions and didn't make a meal out of the physical inspection.'

'How are you paid?'

'In cash by a bloke who comes in at the end of the day's session.'

'How much?'

'It depends on how much I've brought in, but just let me say that it's more than I would be able to earn in any other job in London in the short term without qualifications or references.'

'Any drugs about here?'

The young woman grinned. 'I wouldn't tell you if there were, now would I, but no, there aren't and the woman who gave me the once over looked to see if there was any evidence of injection sites or cocaine use.'

'Well, thank you very much, you've been most helpful. And look after yourself, won't you? What you're letting yourself in for isn't all roses, you know.'

'I know. I can look after myself.'

'That's what they all say.'

Sinclair was deep in thought and didn't say anything until they were within sight of the underground station, then said:

'How about a cup of tea? I'd like to know what you thought of that place.'

'Well,' Sarah said, when they were sitting in

a small café, 'As they go, I'd say it was one of the better ones of that sort. I thought our Aussie friend was perfectly straightforward and a rather upbeat sort of young woman; she genuinely seemed to be enjoying the whole thing and treats sex like a game of volleyball on the beach and I didn't at all get the impression that she was making it up, but there is something distinctly dodgy about that set-up and I worry about her.'

'In what way dodgy?'

'The maid for one thing, not only is her accent phoney as you pointed out, but for another that story about Sophie doesn't ring true. From what you said, the girl didn't even look sixteen and even if she did find out about the place from other drug users, particularly if she had been on the hard stuff, that doesn't tally with what you've been told about her at the school and the lack of evidence of injection marks from the forensic pathologist. What the Australian woman told us also suggests that the people running that flat vet the women they employ quite carefully and surely they would have picked up that Sophie was underage. It also doesn't seem as if they would allow serious sado-masochistic stuff to go on there, either.'

'I agree with all that,' Sinclair said, 'and what also doesn't make sense is why the maid admitted having recognised Sophie. She obviously must know that underage girls are poison in a set-up like that and the most natural and easy thing for her to have done would be to have said she'd never set eyes on her.'

'That's a good point, but it still doesn't explain why Sophie had the number of that place on her mobile, does it? I tell you what, I'll do a bit more digging on that place; I don't promise that I'll be able to come up with anything, but I'll give you a ring anyway.'

'Well, that's very good of you — I appreciate it. I wouldn't have got anywhere near as far without your help and I'm very grateful to you.'

'It's been a pleasure.'

★   ★   ★

Sinclair was not looking forward to his meeting with Watson, which was scheduled for the following afternoon and rather than hang about or have a game of golf in the morning, which would have made him feel guilty, ridiculous though that would have been considering how much extra time he always put in, he decided to see if he could locate Mrs Frampton.

Miss Rainsford was the obvious person to

ask, but she was taking a class and rather than disturb her he walked by the side of the games' field towards the college office. Seeing the gym and swimming pool complex to his left, on a sudden impulse he went in. There were a number of doors leading off the lobby and he stopped outside the one belonging to the office in which he and Fiona had interviewed Jo Roberts earlier. The circular window in the door was covered on the inside by a curtain and when there was no response to his knock, he pushed open the door and went in.

He had hardly taken the room in previously and stood by the open door for a moment, looking around. To his left, there was a desk in front of a large window with a view of the grounds; on it was a computer and to its side a large filing cabinet. A couch covered by a towel was against the wall to the right of it and at its base a trolley with two glass shelves. On these was a collection of medical supplies consisting of crêpe bandages, joint supports, a roll and box of sticking plasters, containers of powder, oils and some paracetamol and arnica. There was a stack of chairs against the wall to the left of the desk and against the one to the right of the entrance was a row of hooks set into a wooden board on which were hanging a white towelling robe and a tracksuit and to its side another small curtain made out of similar material to the one covering the window in the door.

Sinclair was just about to leave when he heard a rhythmical squeaking sound coming from behind it and he lifted one corner of the curtain. There was a rectangle of one-way glass behind it and, moving the curtain slightly, he had a view of the gym. Jo Roberts, whose back was towards him was in a white leotard and was executing a series of graceful somersaults and twists on the trampoline with great height and accuracy hardly moving from the very centre of the apparatus.

Closing the curtain, he made a sudden decision. He took a small bottle and an instrument out of the pocket of the jacket of his suit and working quickly, left the complex immediately he had finished and went straight to the college office.

'Mrs Frampton's address, sir?' the woman behind the desk queried, 'I'm sure we'll have it on our database and I'll have a look for you straight away.'

★   ★   ★

Barbara Frampton had never met a policeman before and she was really excited. The man on the telephone had such a cultured voice and she was flattered that her views on the girls at Sandford College were wanted, though she was shocked and upset to hear that one of them had been found dead in bed and was thought to have taken her own life. Thank goodness nothing like that had ever happened in her own time there. And how awful it must have been for Margaret, whose whole life was the college and particularly the girls in her house.

She said as much to the charming man who had come to see her. He was so nice and had done all the right things; he admired her cottage and the tea set with its silver teapot and had made friends with Tibby, her marmalade cat.

'Yes,' he said, 'I've met Miss Rainsford and she seems a thoroughly nice woman. She is naturally very upset and rather than bother her too much at this difficult time for her, I thought you would be the best person to give me an idea of the sort of pressures the girls are under there. You must have got close to them during your time there.'

'Oh yes, I did. You see I had already had experience of looking after girls, because I was under-matron at a single sex boarding-school for girls after I left school myself and later I became matron proper. That's how I came to meet Jack, who was the doctor there.

When we married, we both so much wanted a family, but sadly it wasn't to be and I kept busy by helping him with his practice, which we ran from our house in those days. He never did take to working with a group of others, which he was more or less forced to do later on and that was made worse by the fact that he wasn't well. At first, no one could put their finger on it, but it turned out to be cancer of the pancreas, such a horrid thing to have, and he died a year later. I was so lucky to get the job at Sandford College; it was a big challenge as they had not taken any girls before and there was a lot of planning to do before the first ones started.'

'Was homesickness a problem for many of them?'

'Yes, particularly as the intake was confined to sixth formers. Girls of sixteen or so are not as adaptable as the younger ones. They are used to freedom; too much of it in my view. Many had boyfriends and found it difficult to settle to communal living. Latterly, things became much better; we learned from our mistakes and the boys got used to having girls about.'

'Did you find it easy to work with Miss Rainsford?'

'Oh, yes. You said that you'd met her?' Sinclair nodded. 'Well, you'll know that

Margaret's a very uncomplicated person, good fun and absolutely fair in her dealings with everyone.'

'Was sex a problem for the girls?'

'Rather less, I think, than for many who are not at boarding-school. I used to talk about it with them and I'm quite sure that my husband was right. He used to say that the majority of young girls who do it just want to keep up with the crowd. They're not as hormone driven as the boys and some of them told me that it was a relief for them to be at Sandford, as the protective environment took a lot of the pressure off them. Several of them even asked me if there was something wrong with them because they didn't want to. Poor dears! I think it was better for a lot of us in the days when we didn't grow up quite so fast.'

'What about drugs?'

'There was none of that in the time I was there, thank goodness.'

'I heard that you had to leave because you had had an accident.'

'Yes, I was going down an escalator in London on the underground; I was just standing there, when one of my legs suddenly seemed to give way and down I tumbled. To this day I can't understand it — I suppose I must have been looking at the advertisements or something and hadn't realised just how close I was to the bottom. I knew straight away that my right hip had gone, the pain was terrible.'

'I can well believe it and such a shock, too. Did anyone stop to help you?'

'It's a sad reflection of the times that you should ask me that, but I can well understand why you do — one does hear such terrible stories, doesn't one? I saw in the paper the other day that a young woman was raped in a passageway off a main street in London and despite her screams nobody moved a finger to help her. Luckily there was this big, rough-looking fellow standing right behind me — all unshaven he was — and he was quite wonderful. I shall never forget him. 'All right, grandma,' he said, 'don't you move and I'll stay with you until the ambulance men come.' He did, too. He made me as comfortable as he could while someone dialled 999. They do have some uses those mobile phones, don't they? I didn't see him go, which was such a pity as I would so like to have written him a note and sent him a present. Perhaps he didn't want a lot of fuss — I expect you come across people like that quite often.'

'Yes, we do. How's your hip now?'

'Wonderful. The whole thing was a blessing

in disguise; I'd been waiting for months for a replacement because of my arthritis and it was done within hours of my accident. I've got no pain at all now and can enjoy long walks again. I did have to give up my job, but I had done it for five years and as the result of all the pain I had, I wasn't really pulling my weight and it was a relief in some ways to give it up. I'm very happy here.'

'I'm so glad.'

'Is there anything else you'd like to know?'

'Did you ever meet your successor?'

'I didn't exactly meet her, I just saw her once at Speech Day during last summer term. Margaret arranged for me to be invited to the big lunch that the governors gave and she performed on the trampoline as part of the gymnastics' display which was put on outside on the games' field. My goodness me, the things she did! It made me quite giddy just watching. I must say that I wondered how good she was with the girls in the house — she is such a severe looking young woman with her hair all cropped — but Margaret did say she was very efficient.' The woman gave a chuckle. 'That's something I could never have been accused of.'

'You would have known Dr McIntosh, of course.'

'I certainly did. He was at medical school

with Jack and he was the one to recommend me for the job as house-mother.'

'What about Mr Hammond?'

'Mr Hammond?'

'He's one of the governors and gave the money for the new gym and swimming pool.'

She gave him a smile. 'I never moved in such exalted circles.'

He was walking back to his car when his mobile phone rang.

'Sinclair.'

'It's Sarah Prescott here. I couldn't help thinking about that place in Earls Court and on the off chance got on to our database to see if there was anything on it. There wasn't, but when I went back there a couple of hours ago, it was locked up and there was no answer to the bell, nor to a phone call ... I happened to catch sight of an old woman at a window in one of the flats opposite; as luck would have it, she turned out to be one those curtain twitchers and said that she'd seen a white van outside the basement flat the previous evening and some stuff had been put in the back by some men in dark boiler suits and hoodies. They didn't take all that much out, but were inside for a good half hour, cleaning up I suppose. I'm afraid there's no way I can take it further without consulting Tyrrell and, knowing him, it would mean

186

clearing it with your Super and I didn't think you would be too keen on that.'

'You a mind reader or something? No, seriously, I'm more than grateful to you and you've given me a good deal to think about. I'll get back to you, if I may, when and, more importantly if, we get to the bottom of it all.'

'I look forward to it. The whole thing is most intriguing and I asked that old duck to keep an eye on it for us, but I reckon the birds have flown.'

9

To Sinclair's relief, Fiona was looking both more cheerful and more animated when he met her two days later.

'I've been having a long think about this case,' he said, 'and if Rawlings is right and Sophie was suffocated, the most likely person to have done it is Jo Roberts. It's quite clear that she had got to know the girl well through swimming and riding and that she had visited her in her bedroom in the evenings on a number of occasions. Now, supposing that she had laced the orange juice with the vodka and rohypnol earlier in the day — it would have been easy enough with the girl in a class and the door of the room not being locked — and then joined her there for a chat that evening. Once she had seen that Sophie had had her drink without noticing anything unusual about it — you remember that Rawlings said that that was a perfectly reasonable possibility — all she would have had to do would have been be to say goodnight and then go back in the middle of the night and plant the vodka, the condoms and the drugs, putting the unconscious girl's fingerprints on the various bottles.

'Perhaps she hoped that the girl would have died as the result of the mixture she had taken, but when she found her still breathing, she decided to suffocate her, say with a pillow. As judged by my experience of the pathologists who stand in for Rawlings from time to time, had one of them done the autopsy, I think that the idea of suicide or an accidental overdose would probably have been accepted.

'Now, what better way to reinforce the idea of suicide than to leave the door bolted on the inside? We know that Jo Roberts is an accomplished gymnast and I reckon she would have been able to climb through the top section of the window, close it up from the outside and then reach the ground by way of the wisteria and the fire escape. Harris did discover that the room had been redecorated for Jo Roberts' use last summer, but she moved out when Sophie arrived and then went into Mrs Frampton's old accommodation, which had been kept for her in case she came back. Perhaps she even rehearsed the climb while she was occupying the room.'

'But what possible motive could she have had for doing something as elaborate as that?'

'Yes, I realise that that is not obvious and that my theory must seem far-fetched and fanciful, but, as you pointed out, Jo Roberts may well be gay and perhaps she tried it on with Sophie and was then threatened with exposure. However, the whole thing seems to me to have been far too premeditated and well-planned to make that credible and yet, if the girl was suffocated, who else could have done it?'

'Rawlings isn't infallible, though, and even admits himself that the coroner would probably not accept his opinion. And what about the window being locked on the inside?'

'That might have been a bit of luck and the icing on the cake as far as Jo Roberts was concerned. She couldn't possibly have known that Miss Rainsford would ask her to wait there to prevent any of the girls from seeing anything after the bolt had been broken and she had gone off to brief the headmaster. When that happened, though, it would have been the work of no more than thirty seconds to nip into the room and push the catch across. What do you think?'

'Very ingenious, but I still can't see a coroner, or even Watson for that matter, buying it.'

'You're probably right, but I think it would be worth getting another view about Jo Roberts from George Farr.'

'The board member who employed Jo Roberts and then recommended her as a replacement for Mrs Frampton?'

'Yes and I've already done a bit of homework on him. He's an Hon, the youngest son of a hereditary peer and by all accounts can be classified as nice, if not exactly dim, although certainly not the brightest spark as far as finance is concerned. The first major problem was some years back with Lloyds, that was hardly his fault, so many other names being caught up in the disaster too, but with help from his family and the sale of some assets, he managed to get going again and was doing all right as a squire with a large country house not far from here and seems to have been quite popular with the locals until he married a model, which did not go down well with either them or his family — evidently she is both vulgar and ostentatious with all sorts of airs and graces and to make matters worse, she proved to be extravagant as well. The final catastrophe occurred when he came a major cropper in one of those dot com fiascos. He's just about managed to hang on to the house, but his office in London has had to go and he has had to move to a small one in Wantage, from which he's now trying to make a go of selling small firs as Christmas trees — one of

191

his few remaining assets is a forest some-where in Scotland. I think a visit to him is the next step so that we can find out how and why he got Jo Roberts on to the staff at the college. We'll have to take it gently because I don't want him to think that we are suspicious of the woman. All right?'

'What line are you thinking of taking?'

'Do you know what Disraeli said to Matthew Arnold about Queen Victoria?'

What on earth was he talking about, Fiona wondered, and decided that the best response would be a shake of the head.

' 'Everyone likes flattery and when you come to Royalty you should lay it on with a trowel.' I think it might be a good idea for us to keep that in mind, even if Farr is only landed gentry. Now, I'm busy this afternoon and I suggest we go in two cars because when we've finished with him I'd like you to pay Mrs Farr a visit and see if you can get another slant on Jo Roberts from her. Softly, softly, would be my advice. Give me a ring this evening and let me know how you got on, would you?'

★   ★   ★

George Farr's office was in a small block in the main street of Wantage, which clearly had only just opened, several of the units still being unoccupied. A fresh-faced and attractive young woman was sitting in the reception area just inside the front door and got up as they went in.

'Mr Farr is expecting you, sir,' she said, in a soft Scottish accent, then walked across to the communicating door and knocked.

George Farr was a tall, spare-framed man with thinning fair hair, probably, Sinclair thought, in his middle forties. He had blue, rather protruding eyes and a fresh complexion.

'I'll do my best to help, Inspector,' he said in his diffident, hesitant voice with its hint of a stammer when Sinclair had explained that they were making enquiries into Sophie Hammond's death. 'Before we start, though, I'm sure you'd both like a cup of coffee. You would? Excellent. I'll just ask Flora to get it for us.'

'You'll have to excuse the lack of organisation and somewhat bare surroundings,' he said when he got back, 'I've only just moved in here and we haven't got things properly sorted yet.'

Comparing the cramped office, with its sparse furniture and cheap carpet, with Hammond's palatial set-up in London, it was only too clear how low the man must have sunk, but Sinclair's fears that they might have to face an inferior brand of instant coffee and powdered milk proved groundless.

'This is really good,' he said, after adding some cream to the fresh brew in a cafetière and taking a sip of the coffee the secretary had brought in.

'I made a resolution that coffee was the one thing that I most definitely wasn't going to economise on,' Farr said with a smile. 'Now, how may I help you?'

'We particularly wanted to see someone of importance about Sophie Hammond, someone who is not on the staff of Sandford College,' Sinclair said, 'and I thought of you, knowing that you had met her and are a member of the board. We have, of course, already spoken to Mr Hammond, but, as I'm sure you understand, we want to bother him as little as possible.'

'Very thoughtful of you,' he said, nodding. 'Only too glad to be of any assistance I can.'

'The board must have been very concerned when they heard the news.'

'They were and I for one was devastated — I couldn't believe it at first. I only met the girl briefly at lunch on a couple of occasions when Derek Hammond asked if Jo Roberts could bring her over to my place to do some riding. I gave Jo a ring and she thought it was a good idea as the girl was lonely and finding it difficult to settle in at the college; she also thought that some fresh air and exercise would be good for her. Sophie was very shy and never said much, but she seemed a nice litte thing; being very polite and she even wrote me a thank you note each time she visited. I can't imagine that teenagers do that very often nowadays. I have known Derek Hammond for years and I very much feel for him — to have your only child take their own life must be terrible, quite terrible.'

'Mr Manners told us that you were able to recommend Jo Roberts to take over from the house-mother of one of the girls' houses when Mrs Frampton had her accident.'

'Yes, I was.'

There was a very long pause, while he fiddled with his teaspoon.

'The fact is,' he said eventually, 'the whole thing was a part of finding a way out of the considerable embarrassment that was facing me.'

'In what way?'

'Well, we live in quite a big place only a few miles from here and a year or so ago my wife decided that she wanted to join one of those fitness clubs that she is always reading about in the women's magazines she used to take. She is a lot younger than I am and was getting concerned about the amount of weight she was putting on. It was nothing to worry about really, but she had decided that her muscles needed to be toned, like the celebrities who feature in the brochures that she sent for. I tried to point out that the results they claimed and the reality were two very different things, but she wouldn't listen and joined one of the most expensive ones in Oxford. I have to admit that I thought that it would be nothing more than one of those passing fads of hers but I couldn't have been more wrong.

'She took it up with real enthusiasm and I was delighted. You see, I worried about her. I used to spend a great deal of time in London on business, too much if the truth be told — and I thought that a real interest in something, particularly when it involved meeting people, was just what she needed. What I hadn't bargained on was that she was finding the journey into Oxford too much and decided that converting the ballroom into a gym and employing a personal fitness trainer would be the answer. I must say I balked a bit at that, but Karen can be very persuasive and, as I said, I was feeling guilty at spending so much time away from her and, in the end agreed to it. She really liked the woman she took on from the club and it is difficult to believe how much her appearance changed. I don't know all the jargon, but she was always talking about 'abs' and 'pecs' and she certainly looked quite marvellous. She also became much more cheerful and it had a very beneficial effect on our marriage, all parts of it, in fact. Then, it all fell apart.'

'In what way?'

The man shook his head and made a gesture at their surroundings.

'Well, you've already seen what I've come to — the problem was that I invested heavily in one of those dot com enterprises which crashed and, as a result I lost a packet. The office in London and my staff up there had to go and I had drastically to reduce the level of domestic help at my house locally; in fact, Mrs Fenton, the housekeeper is the only one left and needless to say, the personal trainer also became a casualty. I did, though, decide to offer Flora a job as my secretary. She's the gamekeeper's daughter from my brother's estate in Scotland and as there was no job for her up there, he asked us to take her on as a sort of au pair, if you like, and offered to cover her salary, which was pretty modest. The agreement was that she should have time off to attend a secretarial course in Oxford and it suited us very well as she was very willing to give Mrs Fenton a hand as things were already getting difficult and I had to get rid of the two housemaids. She did well on the course and when it had ended my brother agreed to pay her a salary as my secretary, which would also have the advantage of giving her some practical experience and a reference in due course when she wanted to move on. She has proved a great success; she has a pleasant manner and in addition to her typing skills, she's good on the telephone. At present, there isn't all that much work for her and she's attending a more advanced computer and word processing course locally. A good friend of mine and his wife are putting her up in return for some baby sitting.'

'So she's not staying with you any more?'

The man suddenly looked up at Sinclair, flushing slightly. 'My wife didn't take to Flora for some reason and wanted her to leave and, rather than have a stand-up row with her and my brother getting involved, I made this arrangement without telling her and she doesn't know about it. I find this intensely embarrassing, but should you decide to see my wife, I'd rather you didn't allude to it.'

'You have no need to worry about that — I quite understand.'

'That's very reassuring — thank you.'

The man wiped his forehead with the silk

handkerchief from the breast pocket of his jacket and there was a long pause before he went on.

'Naturally, I also felt a certain responsibility for Jo Roberts, the personal trainer; she'd given up her previous job at that club to work with Karen and had even moved into our place, but it was Karen's reaction that worried me most — she was absolutely devastated when the young woman had to leave. Luckily, at about the same time, I was at a board meeting at the college and Derek brought up his concerns about the lack of a competent swimming and gymnastics instructor to take advantage of the new facilities that he had financed and which had been completed the previous year. Manners was saying that much though he appreciated what he had said, there was just not enough money to go round to increase the staff.

'I was aware that Derek's daughter was due to start at the college in the autumn and I knew that he was concerned that the house-mother, whom he liked very much when he had gone to inspect the premises, had had an accident and would not be returning. It seemed to me that Jo would be able to fill both posts and that it would kill two birds with one stone and one quick glance towards Derek when I made the suggestion confirmed my belief that he would approve, having met Jo at our place on a number of occasions. Inevitably, one of the other board members brought up the question of the need for an increase in salary for the combined posts and the fact that Jo had no teaching qualifications, but Derek dealt with that by saying that he would have a word with the bursar. That was typical of Derek; he was not the sort of person to make a song and dance about the fact that he was proposing to finance the difference himself, but everyone around the table knew that that was what he was going to do.

'I'm pleased to say that when I asked Guy Manners, the headmaster, how Jo was getting on, he was full of her praises and during the summer holidays she was able to stay with us and had the use of the gym and the pool at the college to keep Karen up to the mark.'

'What did you make of her yourself?'

'I never saw a great deal of her — I was up to my eyes in trying to salvage something from the mess my business had got into while she was staying and before that, she used to come to the house when I was up in London. She was always pleasant to me, though, and used to exercise the horses of my friends, the Calloways, just up the road from us. Their daughter, the one who does the riding, is in

South America doing her gap year. Jo also liked to visit some of the country houses around here as she had undertaken some research for a man writing a history of them and I was able to give her some introductions.'

'Who is the writer?'

'You'll have to ask her about that; she did tell me about it, but the name didn't mean anything to me and I have forgotten it. She's very direct is Jo and she gives Karen her marching orders all right, something I have never achieved.' The man smiled rather wanly. 'I have never been able to stand up to strong women — they've frightened the daylights out of me ever since my prep school days. We had a real dragon of a matron there — no milk of human kindness in her.'

'How are things going now with your new business?'

'Picking up slowly, I'm glad to say. The debts are nearly settled and the current project's looking quite promising; I have to say, though, that none of it would have been possible without Derek Hammond's help.'

'In what way did he do that?'

'Gave me an interest free loan. He even offered to make it a straight gift and although Karen wanted me to accept it, that would have been altogether too much for my self-respect — I couldn't possibly have imposed on him in that way. I can't tell you how relieved I was recently when, having sold some of my land in Scotland, I was able to repay him.'

'Have you known Mr Hammond long?'

'Most of my life. We both went to Sandford College at the same time and I had a great deal to thank him for even then. I was not exactly the right sort of boy for the rather tough school that Sandford was then. To put it bluntly, I was a bit of a wimp and just the sort to get bullied and would have been had it not been for Derek. He wouldn't mind my saying that at that time he had a lot of rough edges — he was one of the scholarship boys that the college took from state schools — but unlike me he was tough, big for his age and the bullies soon discovered just how tough. In return, my parents, after I had told them how good he had been to me and how friendly he was, offered him hospitality. At first, it was just a few Sunday lunches, but then he used to stay with us in the holidays — his mother was a single parent and had to work full time, which was nothing like so common nor so generally accepted as it is now. My father took a particular liking to him and in a very short time, Derek became very much 'to the Manor born'. First of all, he lost his accent, then he excelled at the country pursuits that my father revered so much, such as riding to hounds and shooting, neither of which I either liked or was any good at, and he learned all the social graces. 'He'll go far, that boy,' my father used to say and he was right.'

'What happened to Hammond's mother?'

The man fiddled with his tie. 'She married again and I don't think Derek's seen her for years. For all I know, she may well have died.'

'And Mr Hammond's wife?'

'I've only met her once — the time we went to dinner with them in Esher. I found her rather on the shy side and she didn't say much — perhaps that's not so surprising, Derek does rather tend to hold the floor in company — but she was very pleasant and I can understand why Derek wanted and liked someone such as her at home. He often used to say that going home was like finding an oasis in the desert of his frenetic business life. Those were his exact words and rather a neat way of putting it, I think.'

'Do you know if they had any problems with Sophie? We will, of course, be asking them directly in due course, but I'm sure you'll understand that in tragic circumstances like this, one has to take it very gently.'

The man nodded. 'Can't help you there, I'm, afraid. Derek wasn't one to talk about his home life and it was the same with regard to his many enterprises. Keeps his cards very close to his chest, does Derek.'

George Farr watched through the window as the detectives walked to the car park at the rear of the building. He was conscious that he had told Sinclair a great deal more about his personal life than he had intended, but the man had proved to be so nice and sympathetic and it had been a relief to unburden himself.

*   *   *

Flora McIver had found the job with George Farr excruciatingly boring and what he did sitting in his office all day was a complete mystery to her. He did make a few phone calls, but there was almost no mail and hardly ever any visitors. If it hadn't been for the computer course, her IPod and radio, she would have gone mad. She would have liked to have a word processor to practise on, but Farr had told her that he wasn't able to run to it until the business picked up. What she really wanted to do was get a job in Oxford when the course was over, although she was quite fond of Farr — he was a funny, dry old stick, but he had always been extremely nice to her and she didn't want to let him down, particularly as he had looked after her when the rest of the staff apart from that battleaxe, Mrs Fenton, the housekeeper, had been given the chop.

He had been so nice to her that she even wondered if he was going to try something on, particularly when he had told her not to let either his wife or Mrs Fenton know that she was working for him. How, though, he thought he was going to keep it from them when one of them only had to ring the office to find out, was a mystery to her. For a time, she even tried to put on an English accent when she answered the phone, but the results were so awful even to her own ears, let alone those of the people who rang up, that after a week or two, when there wasn't a single call from the house, she gave it up. Her fears about Farr proved groundless. He remained scrupulously polite and both verbally and physically carefully kept his distance.

The arrival of the two detectives was a welcome diversion and she rather fancied the Inspector, who had a nice smile and had a passing resemblance to Pierce Brosnan. The woman with him wouldn't have been bad looking, either, if she had made more effort with her appearance and hadn't looked such a misery. She couldn't imagine why the police should want to see George, let alone spend so much time with him; perhaps, she thought, he was still in deeper financial trouble than he claimed. She had to admit, though, that he didn't look any different from normal when he saw them off the premises.

'All right if I go out to lunch, Mr Farr?' she asked, a few minutes later.

'Go ahead, m'dear. I'll hold the fort until you get back. Take as long as you like.'

She was standing on the pavement trying to decide between a burger bar and a cheap-looking café and had just decided on the former, taking an instant dislike to the look of the fat, greasy-looking proprietor through the dirty window of the latter, when a voice came from behind her and she whirled round.

'Flora?' It was the tall detective who was smiling at her. 'I wondered if I might have a word with you about Sophie Hammond. Mr Farr may have told you that she was found dead at Sandford College a few days ago.'

Flora felt the blood draining from her face and her hand went to her throat.

'No, he hadn't.'

'Well, as I'm sure you know, we have to look into tragic events like this. Why don't we have something to eat? That pub at the end of the road suit you?'

She nodded and a few minutes later took

him at his word when he told her to order anything she liked, choosing a turkey and leek pie and, greatly daring, a gin and tonic while they were waiting for the food to arrive.

While they were eating, he asked her about herself. He was interested to hear about her plans for the future and how, once she had gained enough experience as a secretary, she hoped to travel and get temporary jobs in somewhere like South Africa or Australia.

It was only after they had finished lunch and were having coffee that he asked her about Sophie.

'Did you see much of her when she visited the Farrs?'

'Hardly at all, really, only when I was serving at lunch. She said almost nothing then and seemed very shy except when she went riding with Miss Roberts, when she was quite different. She always had a bit of colour in her cheeks when they came back and I used to see them chatting together before they took their shower.'

'Shower?'

'Yes, the old ballroom has been converted into a gym and a shower put in one corner. Mrs Farr didn't approve of their using it.'

'Why ever not?'

Flora giggled and blushed. 'Jealous, I reckon.'

'Jealous?'

She looked round. 'Yeah. Mrs Farr and Jo had a thing going when she was staying there. Anyway, I went into the gym the second time Sophie came to visit to see if they were fixed up with towels and I saw her getting into the shower cubicle with Jo.'

'I see. Do you suppose Mr Farr suspected what his wife had been getting up to with Jo?'

'You'd think so, wouldn't you, but nice though he is, he's as thick as two planks, at least that's what I heard Jo say to Mrs Fenton about him one day.'

Sinclair smiled. 'You don't care for Mrs Farr much, do you?'

'I certainly don't. Talk about snooty with her being a dancer in one of those clubs in London before she married George!'

'Who told you that? Mrs Fenton again?'

The young woman nodded. 'The two of them had a big row about something and Mrs Fenton was furious. She called her common as muck and a jumped-up twat amongst other things.'

'I see. What's this Jo like?'

'She's OK. She certainly knew how to get on with George. She pretended to take an interest in his family, the big houses round here and his place in Scotland, which is more than his wife ever did, and he really seemed to come alive with her — it's not surprising, Mrs Farr never seemed to listen properly to anything he said.'

'You said pretended. Why was that?'

'It seemed a strange thing for a woman like her to be interested in and I thought she was just doing it to soften him up a bit. Mrs Fenton told me that George couldn't really afford her salary and was looking for a tactful way to get rid of her.'

'Did Jo ever try anything on with you?'

This time the young women blushed scarlet. 'As a matter of fact she did and at that time not having met all the people of my own age at my course in Oxford, I wouldn't have known how to react had it not been for the agony aunts in the magazines that Mrs Farr used to read and which I was able to rescue from the wastepaper baskets after she had finished with them. I just told her that it wasn't my scene.'

'How did she react?'

'I remember exactly what she replied. 'Pity, I really fancy you. No ill feeling?' '

'And was there?'

'None at all. She never bothered me again and just used to give me a grin whenever we passed each other.'

'How about Sophie? Do you think that that incident in the shower meant all that much?'

'Well, you don't do that sort of thing just to save water, do you?'

'No, I don't suppose you do.'

Flora's hand went to her mouth and she blushed again, but then she saw the detective trying hard not to laugh behind his napkin and began to giggle herself.

'Did Mrs Farr know what happened in the gym?'

'Oh, yes, you should have seen her face when the two of them had gone. She looked as if she was about to have a fit and later I overheard her telling her husband that neither of them were to come near the place again.'

'Which little bird was it that let slip that choice piece of information to her, do you suppose?'

'Not this one, if that's what you're thinking. It must have been Mrs Fenton; she knows everything that goes on in that house. She's been there for ever, long before the Farrs got married and she enjoys stirring things up and sticking the knife into madam. She thinks George needs protecting.'

'How do you know all that?'

'Because she loves a gossip and latterly I was the only audience she had. She also thinks I'm an airhead from north of the border.'

Sinclair took a sip from his coffee cup.

'Would it surprise you if I told you that there's a possibility that Sophie might have taken her own life?'

'I didn't really know her at all — I never even had a proper conversation with her and as I said, she never opened her mouth on either occasion when I was serving at lunch.'

Flora wasn't thinking about Sophie as she walked back to the office, still feeling a bit light-headed from the unaccustomed alcohol, she was thinking about the tall, good-looking man with the beautiful voice and exquisite manners.

★   ★   ★

It was obvious to Fiona from the moment that she drove through the wrought iron gates, one of which was leaning over drunkenly from one hinge, the other having come out of the stone pillar on one side, that Farr's estate was falling or indeed had fallen into considerable disrepair. The rhododendrons were overhanging the drive, there were potholes in the forecourt and the paint was peeling off the window sills.

'I'm DC Campbell,' Fiona said to the rather grim-looking woman in a black dress, who answered the bell. 'Is Mrs Farr in? I'd like to have a word with her.'

'Is it about Sophie?'

'Yes. I imagine you must have seen something of the girl yourself. I gather that she came to lunch here a couple of times.'

'Yes, she did, but I hardly spoke to her. Jo was the one who saw most of her, which didn't exactly please Mrs Farr.'

'Oh, why was that?'

The woman's lips twitched. 'I think you'd better ask her that.'

It was only too clear that Karen Farr had been making serious inroads into the whisky decanter on the table by her side, which was nearly empty, even though it was still early afternoon. The woman with dyed blonde hair, which was black at the roots, was slumped in an armchair. She opened one eye when the housekeeper showed Fiona into the small reception room which looked out on to the park. Mrs Fenton then left abruptly.

'Who the hell are you?'

'Police,' Fiona said firmly.

The woman opened her other eye and squinted myopically at Fiona's warrant card.

'Don't tell me that George has parked on a double yellow line.'

'I'm making enquiries about Sophie Hammond; I'm sure you know that she was found dead in her room at Sandford College last week.'

'Of course I bloody know, George has talked of nothing else since it happened. What's it to do with me?'

'I gather she came to lunch here twice.'

'Only because George was trying to curry favours from Derek Hammond. I hardly spoke to the anorexic little creep, if you must know.'

Fiona pulled up a chair and sat down beside her.

'I understand that Jo Roberts took her riding.'

To Fiona's embarrassment, the woman began to cry silently, the tears running down her cheeks and some moments went by before she got control of herself.

'Jo was supposed to be coming here to help me in the gym and then she had to spoil it all by bringing that brat with her. If I didn't know George so well, I would have thought he was behind it, but he wasn't, it was that two-timing bitch herself.' She gave a loud sniff and blew her nose loudly on the filthy handkerchief, which was on the chair beside her. 'I was so happy here before George lost all his money and the staff were given the push. Can you imagine what it's like here with the winter coming on; it's cold, it's damp and the roof leaks.'

'Why don't you sell it?'

'Well, for one thing George won't let it go and for another no one in their senses would buy it. It's not interesting enough for the National Trust or English Heritage to want it and as it's listed, the developers wouldn't be allowed to pull it down.'

'How about a health farm? I gather you've already got a gym here.'

'That's the one part of the building that's in good condition and I had to sweat blood to get it. George can be very stubborn, you know.'

'May I have a look at it?'

For the first time since Fiona had been there, the woman's face showed a measure of animation and with considerable difficulty she got to her feet and stood there swaying.

'You'll have to help me — I've not been well, you know.'

The former ballroom must have been a good sixty feet long and some twenty-five wide and there were windows, all fitted with blinds, along the whole of one side giving views of the rose garden, which like everything else in the place was in need of attention. The wooden floor had been covered by a kind of slightly springy composition and dotted around were various pieces of muscle strengthening apparatus: a rowing machine; a trampoline; a treadmill and a massage table.

'I suppose the bathrooms are a long way from here,' Fiona said, pointing towards the large, glass fronted shower cubicle.

'Bloody miles,' the woman replied, 'and most of it along draughty corridors. The boilers in this place are a major explosion waiting to happen and that's why that thing's got its own heating element.'

'Did you know Jo Roberts well?'

'Don't speak to me about that bitch — she let me down badly.'

'Oh, in what way?'

'What's it to you?' The woman squinted at her. 'I thought you said you were enquiring about Sophie Hammond.'

'Jo Roberts appears to have been looking after her at the college and I was just interested to know what you thought of her.'

'Well, you can take your interest elsewhere; looking after the girl is hardly the words I would use to describe what she was doing.'

'I don't follow you.'

The woman gave a snort of derision. 'I'm not surprised. Now push off, will you, or else I'll get George to have a word with Hastings — I suppose you know who he is? And perhaps you also know what the word harassment means?'

Fiona had had enough, finding her own way out of the house and spinning the wheels of the car and sending up a shower of loose gravel as she accelerated violently down the drive. God, she thought, yet another failure and what was she going to tell Sinclair when she telephoned him that evening?

'I'm afraid it was a wasted visit,' she said when she had described the place to him and that the woman was both tipsy and uncooperative.

'Not to worry. I wasn't expecting it to be particularly rewarding, but it does give me a clear picture of what it must be like there. It also confirms my belief that Jo Roberts was providing rather more than comforting words and encouragement to Sophie. Anyway, I've got to meet Watson tomorrow, not something I'm looking forward to, and so I'll see you at the office the day after.'

10

Bill Watson had had a distinctly sticky fifteen minutes with Hastings, the Chief Constable, on the telephone earlier that morning and was not in a good mood when Sinclair arrived.

'He can't understand why the inquest has been put off for so long and neither can I for that matter,' he said. 'The other thing that's got him worried is that before long rumours are going to start flying around. I know that Rawlings thinks that the girl was suffocated and that he's very seldom wrong, but even he admits that there's no evidence that any self-respecting coroner would accept. An open verdict is never very satisfactory at inquests, but it's as clear as daylight to me after what you've told me and from what I've read in Harris's report that it was either an accident, being an extreme reaction to the drugs the girl had taken, or suicide. We'll just have to hope that the sordid details are kept to an absolute minimum. And how do you suppose Hammond's going to react if Rawlings gets too fanciful about that suffocation theory of his? He's just the sort of man who'll insist on a second autopsy by his own man and, what's more would pay for it. What more would anyone want, for God's sake? There is strong evidence that the girl had been taking drugs, had been involved in a particularly sordid and unpleasant form of prostitution to pay for it and was known to be depressed and withdrawn. And how did Rawlings's murderer get into the girl's room? Telekinesis or whatever the bloody term is?'

'I knew you'd be worried, sir, and that's why I went to see Rawlings yesterday.'

'And?'

'He's in the process of doing one last test and he promised me the results later today.'

'What sort of test?'

'He wouldn't say, but he clearly thought that it was of great importance. If he is right about suffocation — and I have seldom if ever known him wrong about something like that — there is only one person in my view who could have done it and that is Jo Roberts.'

'What? The house-mother?'

Sinclair nodded, 'Let me explain.'

He put his theory to his superior in almost exactly the same way as he had to Fiona. Watson listened to him without interrupting until he had finished.

'All right,' he said, 'I grant you that what you say would have been possible, but do you see the coroner buying it? As you well know, he works on facts, not theories. In my view, the whole idea's too fanciful by half. What do you know about this woman and what motive could she have had?'

'Very little so far. We found several sets of fingerprints in the girl's room, including hers, but she was often in that room as part of her job and there was no match for them on the national database. She was working as a personal trainer for Mrs Farr before she went to Sandford — she's the wife of George Farr, a local landowner, one of the governors of the college and a friend of Derek Hammond. That arrangement hit the buffers when he lost a packet in a dot com fiasco. There is also a suggestion that the woman was being rather more than just a house-mother to Sophie.'

'Good God! And where did that nugget come from?'

'Mrs Farr. She claims that when Sophie went to their house on a few occasions to have Sunday lunch and go riding with Jo Roberts, rather more than riding went on.'

'How reliable is the woman?'

'Not very. She's a drinker, she hasn't adjusted to the dramatic change in her life style now that money is short and it appears that she was closer to Jo Roberts than she should have been. 'Heav'n has no rage, like love to hatred turn'd, nor Hell a fury, like a woman scorn'd' '

'You mean that Mrs Farr and this woman had been having it off together and that she was jealous of the Hammond girl?' Sinclair nodded. 'Well, why not bloody well say so and spare me the clever, clever stuff.'

'I'm sorry, sir.'

'Well, come along man, have you any solid evidence for what sounds to me like pure conjecture?'

'Both the housekeeper and the girl who had been their au pair also hinted at it.'

'Hmm. Well, all I can say is that you'd better be careful not to spread rumours like that unless you've got more than hints to go on.'

'I had no intention of doing so, sir. It was just for your ears and I thought you should know about it.'

'All right, all right. I'll do my best to pacify Hastings, but unless something impressive comes up in the next twenty-four hours, that inquest will have to go ahead. As you know, he's also on the board of Sandford College with Hammond and I'm sure you can understand that we can't go on stalling forever.'

'Yes, I do realise that, but if this Jo Roberts has done it and she gets to know of our suspicions and does a runner, think how that would make us look.'

'Your suspicions, you mean. If I read you aright, you are hinting that Hastings might not be as discreet as you would like. How would you like it if say DC Campbell hinted to me the same thing about you? You wouldn't, would you? If Hastings were to hear the faintest whisper of what you're implying, you'd be off the case in no time flat and you'd better bear that in mind. Now, you're not to do anything further without my say-so and you're to report Rawlings's findings on this test of his to me as soon as it's through. Is all that quite clear?'

'Yes, sir.'

★   ★   ★

It was late afternoon when Rawlings rang Sinclair on his mobile.

'Would you come over right away? I'd rather not speak about it over the phone?'

Sinclair knew better than to ask the man any more questions and was there inside fifteen minutes. 'I'm rather concerned about young Fiona Campbell,' Rawlings said. 'I think she's identifying rather too closely with this Sophie Hammond.'

'In what way?'

'Child abuse and all that. She obviously thinks that that explains the girl's behaviour and . . .'

'And you consider that she might have been a victim of that, herself, too?' Rawlings nodded. 'I have had similar thoughts myself. You see, I don't believe that she's cut out for this type of police work; there's no question about her dedication or her ability, but she takes it all too personally. I have very real concerns for her, but for the life of me I can't think what I can usefully do about it. She gets teased enough as it is by the coarser members of our force, 'Saint Fiona of Falkirk', 'Tin Knickers of Troon' are two of the milder sobriquets I have overheard recently and if it became known that we suspect that she had been abused herself at some time in the past, I hate to think what might result from that.'

'Any chance of her moving sideways into an area of police work that's less upsetting for someone of her background and in which she's less vulnerable to male aggression?'

'I think that would be an excellent solution, but unfortunately my standing with the powers that be is sinking by the day.' Sinclair cleared his throat. 'I don't suppose, though, that you asked me over here just to discuss that.'

The pathologist looked across the desk at

the detective over the top of his half moon glasses. 'No, I didn't, but I thought I'd mention it none the less.' There was a long pause. 'In March of last year,' he continued, 'the middle-aged owner of a country house near Stow-on-the-Wold in Gloucestershire was found battered to death in her drawing-room. It appears that she had had one or two whiskies too many and instead of going to bed, had switched out the light and gone to sleep in a high-backed armchair by the fireplace. An intruder got in by cutting a hole in the dining-room window and then went into the drawing-room in order to steal a collection of netsuke in a display cabinet. I take it that you know what that is?'

'Yes. Small Japanese ivory or wooden carved objects. They're very valuable if of the right age and the quality of the carving is exceptional.'

'Exactly and that's what they were. There were also some Fabergé ornaments and jewellery on the shelf above. The owner, whom the burglar had clearly failed to see, was evidently a woman of considerable spirit, if not of equal prudence, because she picked up a heavy silver candlestick from the mantelpiece and clobbered the robber with it. Unfortunately, the blow was neither hard enough, nor accurate enough to disable the burglar, who hit the woman on the side of the head with a heavy glass paperweight. It was no mean blow, shattering the temporal bone and killing her instantly. The servants were awakened by the sound of the display cabinet hitting the floor and found the poor woman lying dead on the floor and the butler made a 999 call. It was answered in today's somewhat tardy fashion — in rather over thirty minutes, I gather — and by then the burglar had long gone. No fingerprints or other clues were found apart from the vital one of the bloodstains and some black wool fibres on the base of the candlestick, the stem of which was still clasped in the dead woman's hand.'

'And the DNA matched that from those hairs I gave you?'

'As ever, my dear Sinclair, you don't disappoint me. Yes, I have made a few more enquiries and that particular robbery has been linked with a whole series of others in that part of the country and not only there. It has been a feature of them, although not in this case, that they have often occurred when the house owners have been holding a party, a dance or a large dinner party, when security has been lax and alarms not set. There has also been evidence that access has been gained by daring climbs in through upper windows. On the last occasion, though, there was no alarm system. The owner was something of an eccentric and didn't approve of such modern fads.'

'That really puts the cat amongst the pigeons.'

'Enlighten me, my dear fellow.'

Sinclair told the pathologist about the uncomfortable interview he had had with his superior and his reasons for concluding that Jo Roberts must have been the one to suffocate Sophie Hammond.

'You see, I was so angry at the way that Watson was so obviously covering his back with the Chief Constable that, rather than hanging around the station waiting for your call, I drove up to Bicester and was able to check on what Jo Roberts told when I first met her, that the white patch of hair on the crown of her head had been due to being mugged in the town and that she had been taken to the hospital by a passer-by.'

'And the date?' Rawlings let out a low whistle when Sinclair told him. 'The same as the robbery. Game set and match. And what ingenious theory do you have for her motive for killing the girl?'

Rawlings let out a low whistle when Sinclair explained.

'That certainly does complicate the issue. What are you going to do now?'

'I know what I'd like to do and that's to arrest the woman as soon as possible, but if I want to stay on the case, or keep my job for that matter, I'll have to speak to Watson about it first.'

'Are you worried about her doing a runner?'

'Yes, but only if she finds out that we're on to her — that's why I didn't want Watson talking about it to anyone, not even to Hastings.'

'Would it help if I gave Watson a call?'

Sinclair pursed his lips. 'I think it would. If I told him, he'll be bound to ask how you got hold of the specimen of DNA and he's such a stickler for the rules that it would be yet another nail in my coffin if he knew that I had lifted some hairs from Roberts's tracksuit top.'

'Worry not, my dear fellow. Leave it to me.'

He lifted up the telephone and pressed one of the bars at its base.

'Get me Chief Superintendent Watson, would you please, Miss Ryle? I need to speak to him now, wherever he is and whatever he's doing. Is that clear?'

The pathologist gave Sinclair one of his special twisted smiles when the call was put through a few minutes later.

'Watson!' he bellowed. 'Rawlings here.'

He delivered a succinct summary of the information he had obtained about Jo Roberts and then raised his eyebrows as he listened to what the man said in reply.

'Look here, Watson, do you seriously expect me to go into that sort of detail now? Just be thankful that you've got the information ... Of course I'm sure, man. And now will you believe that that girl Sophie Hammond was murdered and are you going to have that woman Roberts arrested? ... I see. Well, if she takes a powder, to use an admittedly rather nasty Americanism, on your head be it.'

Rawlings gave a grunt of satisfaction when he had rung off.

'That should settle the bugger's hash, but I wouldn't bet on it. Rules, rules, rules, that's all he ever thinks about. He wanted to know how we connected the DNA to the Roberts woman and, as you heard I sidestepped that, but then he said: 'Of course, I'll have to check with the Chief Constable first.' God!'

'So he's not prepared to authorise the woman's arrest today?'

'It seems not, but this clever machine of mine has recorded our conversation if some further tail twisting is required later on.'

Bad though Rawlings's imitation of Watson had been, Sinclair couldn't keep the grin off his face and he left in the best humour he had been in for days.

★　★　★

Sinclair was having breakfast the following morning when the phone rang.

'Guy Manners, here. More bad news, I'm afraid. Jo Roberts was found drowned in the pool about about twenty minutes ago; her body was discovered by one of the boys.'

'I'll come right away.'

The detective abandoned his meal, rang Fiona and picked her up at her flat a short time later.

'I was afraid something like this might happen,' he said, when they were in the car and he had explained his hunch that DNA findings might possibly turn up something on the woman and that these had in fact proved that she was the country-house robber. 'Perhaps I should have pushed Watson harder about arresting her yesterday.'

'Suicide, do you think?'

'Possibly and, if so was it because she had got to hear that we were on to her and about to arrest her?'

'But how could she have known that?'

'I gather that Hastings was at a board meeting at the college yesterday evening after

Watson had spoken to him and just possibly he relayed the information about Jo Roberts to Manners or one of the board members and that's how it got out.'

By the time they reached the college and had been taken to the pool by the Headmaster, Rawlings was already there, on his knees by the body.

'Ah, Sinclair, up bright and early, I see. So, she or someone else beat you to it, eh?' The pathologist saw Manners' puzzled look and slowly got to his feet. ''Fraid I won't be able to tell you anything much until I've done the autopsy.'

Manners nodded. 'I expected that.'

'Who was it who found her?' Sinclair asked.

'Young Preston — I think you know who he is.' Sinclair nodded. 'Pickering, his house-master, is looking after him at the moment and I expect you'd like a word with him. I gather from the man that Preston was very upset by Sophie Hammond's death. Her death and now this one will no doubt have shaken him profoundly, particularly as he found the woman lying on the bottom of the pool. It's not up to me to tell you how to handle him, but you will go easy, won't you?'

'Of course I will, don't worry. It'll only be very brief; I just want to know how he found her and what he did after that. If he wants his house-master to be there when I talk to him, that's fine by me. Fiona, perhaps you'd stay with Dr Rawlings if he doesn't object. It'll be good experience for you.'

Fiona wasn't fooled for one minute. Sinclair knew as well as she knew herself that she had made a mess of her interview with Preston before and it was hardly surprising that he didn't want her there. As for Rawlings, had Sinclair been talking to him about her and was that why the pathologist had made his approach to her on the previous weekend? It wouldn't have surprised her; if this were the case and she did decide to take up Rawlings's offer, it would certainly make things easier for her. Further thoughts or speculation were abruptly cut off by Rawlings's penetrating voice.

'Right, Miss Campbell, what am I looking for?'

Had the pathologist really given her a wink as the others turned away? She was pretty certain that he had and did her best to answer sensibly.

★　★　★

Rob Preston was sitting in his house-master's living-room cradling a mug of cocoa and even though he had had a hot shower, as hot as he could bear it, he still shivered from time to time, unable to get the images from the swimming pool out of his mind.

'Hello.'

He whirled round, not having heard the door open, then started to get up as he saw the tall, pleasant-looking man, who was advancing towards him smiling.

'Don't get up,' he said. 'I'm Mark Sinclair, you may have seen me around.'

'You're the detective?'

'Yes, that's right. Don't worry though, all I need is a first-hand account of how you found Miss Roberts. Of course, I realise that the last thing you want just now is someone like me descending on you when you have had such a shock, but I'm sure you realise how necessary it is. Do say if you'd like your house-master to be here, or even the Head.'

Unlike the miserable-looking woman who had made those unpleasant insinuations about him and Sophie and to whom he had taken an instant dislike, he didn't find the detective in the least threatening.

'No, that's all right.'

The man nodded. 'Perhaps you'd start by telling me how you came to find her? Take your time, there's no hurry.'

* ★ ★ ★

Rob Preston glanced at his watch as he approached the gym complex. He was twenty minutes late, having slept through his alarm and was feeling heavy-headed and sluggish. He was bound to get a bollocking from the woman, whom he hadn't been able to look at without revulsion ever since he had seen what she had been doing to Sophie. It wasn't only that. Even in the short time he had known her, he had, in his own way, worshipped the girl. She had seemed so quiet, so nice and so innocent. And yet she had let Miss Roberts do those things to her and the bitterest blow had come when that wretched policewoman had mentioned the condoms found in Sophie's room. He hadn't considered for one moment that any of the boys at the college would have even thought about her in that way, let alone have done anything about it. If he found out who it was, he was going to kill them and what about Jo Roberts? She didn't deserve to live, either. Before he had seen what the woman was capable of doing to Sophie, he had admired her for her diving and trampoline skills and even used to arrive early for the early morning training sessions so that he could watch her carrying out her regular practice routine. Now, he couldn't

232

bear the sight of her. Why then, he thought, had he continued to torture himself by turning up regularly? The answer to that was simple; if he hadn't, like as not it would have led to further questioning and that creepy policewoman making further insulting insinuations.

He pushed at the door, knowing that he would never be able to do anything about Jo Roberts and praying that the door would be locked. It wasn't and he pushed it open and when he heard no sounds from the pool, he knocked on the door of her office and then opened it when there was no reply. The woman's clothes were laid out on the couch, with her watch beside them and he turned, pushed open the swing door to the pool and walked in. He saw the shape lying on the bottom of the deep end at once and instinct taking over he didn't hesitate, dropping the bundle of his trunks and towel and after a few short running steps, he entered the water in a shallow dive.

He didn't waste time in trying to get her out by the nearest steps at the deep end but taking a firm grip under her shoulders, he kicked hard backwards until he was able to stand and then dragged her up the steps at the shallow end of the pool.

He had done a life-saving course and had

even worked as a guard on one of the surfing beaches in Cornwall during the previous summer holidays and put all he had learned into practice; he forced what water he could from her mouth and nose, he tried mouth to mouth respiration and then, unable to feel her pulse, he started external cardiac massage and when all that had failed, he lifted her up by her ankles, trying to drain some of the water out of her air passages. Even then he didn't give up, trying the entire sequence again. None of it was of any use; Jo Roberts was dead.

★   ★   ★

'You clearly did absolutely everything possible,' Sinclair said, 'no one could have done more. What do you think happened to her?'

'She must have hit her head on the edge of the springboard; you see, there was a nasty cut on her scalp.'

'I didn't know that springboard divers were at risk from that.'

'Yes, they are, but only the real experts. I've even seen it happen on a video that my father gave me that featured famous swimmers and divers. An American called Greg Louganis was doing a reverse two and a half somersaults in the pike position at the Seoul

Olympics, misjudged the initial jump and hit his head on the edge of the board. He wasn't knocked out, but had a bad cut on his head and there was a bit of a flap because he was HIV positive.'

'Was Miss Roberts capable of doing dives like that?'

'Oh yes, she was really good and always used to practise before Sophie and I arrived in the morning.'

The young man's voice had cracked and he looked down, but then quite suddenly raised his head and looked the detective straight in the eye.

'I was very angry and upset when your assistant suggested that I was having sex with Sophie. The main reason was that it wasn't true, but that wasn't all.'

He told Sinclair what he had seen in Jo Roberts' office and how let down he had felt by Sophie, but even more than that by Jo Roberts.

'I realise now that I had no real cause to be angry with Sophie; after all, although she was friendly, she never gave me the slightest encouragement, but Miss Roberts was on the staff and she took advantage of a girl who was clearly innocent, lonely and shy. I did my best, though, for her, I really did.'

'There can be no doubt about that. Now,

you may well be asked to make a written statement about how you found Miss Roberts and what you did to try to resuscitate her, but just stick to that. Don't offer an opinion about how she came to be under the water, nor mention what you've just told me — I'll take care of that. All right?' The young man nodded. 'Cheer up; you've had a really nasty experience, but you can be proud of the way you coped.'

Rob Preston sat there until his house-master's wife looked in to see him and asked how he was getting on.

'I'm fine, thank you, Mrs Pickering.'

'Why not stay here until lunch — there are plenty of magazines and tapes over there.'

'It's very kind of you, but I'd like to go to my next class.'

The woman smiled. 'I'm sure you know what's best for yourself, but don't hesitate to come for a chat if you feel the need — any time.'

★ ★ ★

Sinclair had seldom in his life been more angry than when he left Rob Preston and was walking towards the college office. Watson must have told someone about his suspicions of Jo Roberts, presumably Hastings, and, walls having ears, the person behind all this had also heard of it and decided that the house-mother should be eliminated.

The same woman who had given him Mrs Frampton's address was in the college office and smiled as the detective walked in.

'I expect you've already heard about Miss Roberts's tragic accident,' he said. The woman nodded. 'I wonder if I might look at her personal file; I am anxious to trace her next of kin and I don't want to bother Mr Manners at a time like this. I won't need to take it away.'

'Of course, sir.'

As Sinclair had expected there was no mention of any next of kin and the document was very short only containing details of her two previous jobs, a glowing reference from George Farr and a briefer but equally good one from one Julia Cairns, the senior physiotherapist at a health club in North Oxford. Personal details were scant in the extreme and apart from her age and earlier employment with a stunt school near Bicester, there was merely the standard disclosure check for working unsupervised with children, which was negative. There were no details of her family, schooling or religious affiliation.

'Do you have a record of the people who were on her appointment committee?'

'I'll look in the file for you, sir.' She took a volume from the shelf to the side of her desk and flicked through the pages. 'Yes, here we are. Mr Manners was in the chair and the others present were the Hon. George Farr, who is a member of the board, Dr McIntosh and Miss Rainsford.'

'Were any special comments made?'

'Some reservations were expressed about Miss Roberts's lack of experience in a school, but the members were impressed by her expertise in gymnastics and swimming and her willingness to supervise in those areas. It was decided to appoint her for one year in the first instance with a review of her performance at the end of it with a view to making a permanent appointment if she proved satisfactory. Mr Farr indicated that she had made a very favourable impression on him and his wife and her excellent reference from the health club was also noted.'

After thanking the woman, Sinclair was on the point of driving to the health club when his phone rang.

'Watson here, I want to see you right away and that means dropping whatever you are doing. Understood?'

'Yes, sir.'

Sinclair had a shrewd idea what was going to happen and one look at his superior's face was enough to confirm it.

'I accept that the Roberts woman was the burglar responsible for that robbery in Gloucestershire last year, but what has that to do with Sophie Hammond's death? As far as I can see, there isn't a shred of evidence that she killed the girl and as for yours and Rawlings's cock-eyed theories that the woman was murdered, words fail me. You're off the case until the inquests are both over and I'll discuss the whole matter with you then. As for that robbery, that's in the hands of the people who investigated it before and you're not to stick your nose into that and the same goes for DC Campbell. Is that absolutely clear?'

For one moment Sinclair thought of telling the man that he was convinced that Jo Roberts's position as a house-mother at the college had been engineered and that the people running both the health club and the stunt school where the woman had worked previously should be investigated further, but quickly changed his mind when he saw the expression on the man's face.

'Yes, sir,' he said.

* * *

'Don't tell me, Jo Roberts hit her head on the diving board, knocked herself out and drowned as a result.' Sinclair said when he had gone to Rawlings's office to hear the result of the autopsy.

The pathologist raised his eyebrows. 'Do you have second sight as well as your other talents, my dear Sinclair?'

The detective grinned. 'No, but I did have a most informative chat with young Preston the morning it happened and he enlightened me on the subject of advanced springboard diving.'

Rawlings listened carefully while Sinclair repeated the young man's account of what had happened to the American Olympic diver.

'Very interesting. And so you would expect there to have been bloodstains on the edge of the board in this case, too?'

'I would be very surprised had there not been, but I don't believe that this was an accident and I have great respect for the expertise of the person or persons who killed her. I don't think they would have neglected to provide that piece of evidence, because, if I'm right, they clearly wanted to make it look like a diving error.'

'And what's your view of this conspiracy theory, Miss Campbell?'

'I agree that her death's highly unlikely to have been an accident, but I think Rob Preston must be the prime suspect,' Fiona said. 'After all, despite his denials I still think he was having sex with Sophie; there were the condoms in her room and if he was in love with her and then he found out that she had been seduced by Jo Roberts, might he not have killed them both?'

'I grant you that that is not a wholly unreasonable suggestion,' Sinclair said, 'but, having seen him I am quite sure that he is too broad shouldered to have been able to climb out of Sophie's window and also think it highly unlikely that a schoolboy, even one who is seventeen, would act in such a premeditated and deliberate way over both deaths. In my view, the case is a good deal more complex than that. I'll explain shortly, but I'd like to hear the post-mortem results first.'

Rawlings who had been watching the two detectives with considerable interest, although he was careful not to make it obvious, nodded.

'This young woman did indeed die as the result of drowning; there was also extensive bruising of the anterior part of her chest wall and several fractured ribs, which occurred post mortem and were presumably due to the distinctly enthusiastic efforts of the boy at cardiac resuscitation. A cut and bruise were also present on her scalp at the back of her head and, as you surmised, blood of the same group was found on the edge of the springboard.

'Interestingly, too, there was a scar on her scalp with that patch of white hair over it that you told me about and a small depressed fracture of the vertex of her skull beneath, which fits in nicely with the DNA findings at the scene of that country house murder. As for the rest, she was otherwise fit, but you may be interested to know that she was not a virgin; however, in the present social climate one has to consider the possibility that penetration might have been due to a sex toy, rather than natural means. There is one other interesting crumb of information.'

'What's that?'

'A bottle was found in the woman's office and it contained an interesting drug that is not at all easy to come by. It's called gamma hydroxybutrate, GHB or Liquid X. It is another of the so-called date rape drugs, causing excitement and purportedly acting as an aphrodisiac. Now, why not fill us in on your grand theory and Miss Campbell and I will act as devil's advocates.'

'Very well,' said Sinclair after a long pause during which he marshalled his thoughts.

'The first thing I would like to consider is the enigma posed by Sophie. How does one equate Miss Rainsford's view of her as a shy, over-conscientious sixteen year-old who was an excellent rider and an even better swimmer, with the drug-addicted, promiscuous psychopath suggested by the drugs and the condoms in her room, let alone the prostitute story? I don't think one can and I'll come to that later. Now, if one assumes that Sophie was suffocated, I am convinced that Jo Roberts did it. How might she have set about it? Picture the scene: she goes to Sophie's room that evening, as she had done often enough before — we know that they were getting on well together — she chats to her and, having doctored the orange juice with vodka and the drugs earlier in the day, she pretends to share a drink with her. Having tucked the girl up in bed and said goodnight, she departs knowing that Sophie doesn't bolt the door at night, it being against the rules and Sophie, not being one of the world's rebels, is highly unlikely to have done so in any case, let alone if she was drowsy and settled in bed.

'The Roberts woman comes back in the middle of the night, no doubt expecting to find Sophie dead and when she discovers that although deeply unconscious, the girl is still breathing, she suffocates her, using the minimum degree of force necessary and when she is satisfied that she really is dead, she carefully tidies the bedclothes, plants the condoms, cocaine and other drugs then leaving by the window after bolting the door. For someone like her, a gymnast and a cat burglar, it would have been child's play to close the window behind her, make the traverse along the wisteria and go down the fire escape. She would have no doubt looked upon it as a bonus that Miss Rainsford should put her on guard outside the room the following morning and the work of a moment to lock the sash window and return to her post. Fortunately for us, by doing that and ignoring King John's advice that 'To gild refined gold, to paint the lily' and so on, would be a 'wasteful and ridiculous excess', her actions made it clear to us that if you were right, Rawlings, Jo Roberts must have done the suffocating. Are you with me so far?'

The pathologist nodded. 'Any comments, Miss Campbell, apart from wonder at your superior's skill with the apt quotation? I shall have to watch my step after that and what my wife said the other day, which was: 'when will you get it into your head that people get bored by listening to your boasting about your literary skills and classical education, real or imagined?' Ouch!'

Not for the first time, Fiona had not the least idea what the man was talking about it and decided to ignore it.

'I agree that if that woman hadn't locked the window, Inspector Sinclair probably wouldn't have considered her to be the number one suspect for Sophie's murder.'

'As usual, my dear, you go straight to the nub of things and it sounds to me as if you're still not wholly convinced. Tell us more, my dear fellow.'

'Let me consider Jo Roberts in more detail, first,' Sinclair continued. 'Why does a young woman who has been a gymnast, a diver, stuntwoman, personal trainer and, for good measure a cat burglar, want to become a house-mother at a public school? The why might be explained by her serious head injury during that burglary and that as a lesbian, with a particular penchant for adolescent girls, she jumped at the opportunity to work with that age group and combine it with swimming and gymnastic instruction. The whole set-up, though, may well have been more calculated than that. Did someone suggest, or perhaps even order, her to hone her climbing skills at that stunt school, where I discovered she had been employed before the health club, in order to make her an even more effective cat burglar? After her injury did she cultivate Mrs Farr and persuade her to take her on as a personal trainer in her house, knowing that it would give her the opportunity to get information about country houses and their owners? Now, disposing of the sort of things that were stolen would, I think, require contacts and special knowledge that she would have been highly unlikely to possess. This again points to direction from someone else, not to mention the attempt to provide her with an alibi at the hospital in Bicester.'

'That first bit I can understand,' said Fiona, 'but how about the move to Sandford College?'

'George Farr's finances were beginning to collapse last summer and did Jo Roberts' director of operations see this as a golden opportunity to use the man, who clearly is not the brightest of sparks, to help her to get information about local country houses in order to facilitate her burgling opportunities and to further his other plans for disposing of Sophie, particularly as at that time the woman had probably had to suspend her robberies following her head injury?'

'Did Mrs Farr say anything more to you about Jo Roberts, Miss Campbell?' Rawlings asked.

'No she didn't, but that's not surprising. She had clearly become intensely jealous on account of Jo's interest in Sophie and obviously didn't want to talk about her at all, let alone in any detail.'

'Right, carry on, Sinclair.'

'Now, if I am right so far, what was Jo Roberts's motive for killing Sophie? I don't believe she had one, I think she was ordered to do it and if Sophie's death was put down to suicide or an accidental overdose, no doubt she would have melted away after a reasonable period of time. It didn't occur to me, until you mentioned the Liquid X, that possibly the shadowy figure behind all this didn't know that Roberts had fallen for Sophie in a big way and that she was using drugs, including the rohypnol and Liquid X to have her way with the girl. You see, Rob Preston told me that he had witnessed the woman giving Sophie a distinctly intimate massage in her office and that it was in no way resisted. Why was that, when Sophie seemed so shy and inhibited? I suspect that it was partly due to the drugs and the fact that someone had at last shown an interest in what she was doing, both in the swimming pool and with her project and, having been starved of affection for so long, it is not so surprising that initial physical contacts should have been accepted and the rest followed on from that. However, when whoever is behind all this realised that we were on to Roberts and about to arrest her, the decision must have been taken to eliminate her as soon as possible. And how was that information discovered? Hastings must have talked to someone at the board meeting, possibly the headmaster, and been overheard. Who, then, do you suppose might have had a motive for blackening Sophie's character, killing her and setting up such an elaborate way of doing it?'

'Hammond,' Fiona said suddenly.

'Exactly. First, let me deal with the reasons for thinking that. Who arranged for Sophie to go to Sandford College? Who suggested to his friend, George Farr, that Jo Roberts would be the ideal person to replace the retired house-mother, who had had such a convenient accident on an escalator, and who had enough clout to set up the smear on Sophie's character with that prostitute business, even to the extent of putting the phone number of the place in Earls Court on her mobile, which might so easily have misled us?'

Rawlings stroked his chin. 'But why such an elaborate charade and what might his motive have been?'

'I believe that Hammond is a control freak

and likes nothing better than to pull the strings, probably of all sorts of illegal activities and I think you, Fiona, know what his motive was.'

'Yes, I do. Hammond had been abusing Sophie sexually.'

'And why, do you suppose, did she never tell anyone in order to put a stop to it?' Rawlings asked.

Fiona looked at the two men one after the other straight in the eye and made a sudden decision.

'I know about sexual abuse, you see, because it happened to me. I never told anyone about it either, until my stepfather was arrested on a charge of GBH after a drunken brawl in a pub and I was bullied into it by the social workers. And why were they so keen to prove it? I believe it was because it had become the flavour of the moment — it was the time of that Satanic abuse stuff — and they had a mission to uncover it.'

'Like witch finders, you mean?' Rawlings said.

'Exactly. I wished to God they had left me alone; I've been suspicious of social workers and counsellors ever since. It was so humiliating; it wasn't just every sordid detail that they dragged out of me, but the medical examination — you may not believe it, but they held me down while they did it. And why did I keep it to myself for so many years? It was because there was no one I was able to trust; my mother was seriously ill when it started, I didn't want to make things worse for her by adding to her misery and after she died, I was terrified of what my stepfather would do to me if he found out that I had been talking, say, to one of the teachers at my school. In some ways I was lucky; had it not been for my uncle and aunt, who took me away and were quite wonderful, I might well have killed myself and it wasn't until my stepfather died in prison that I at last had some peace of mind.

'So you see, I can understand why Sophie didn't tell her mother or anyone else. At least my stepfather was a drunkard and had had a rotten upbringing himself, but Hammond is a very different proposition. I believe that he frightened her into silence and in that case, why did he decide to kill her? Perhaps pre-adolescent girls were his thing and he may have lost interest in her. Perhaps he was worried by the change in the social scene, believing that even at this late stage she might suddenly take the decision to report him; I don't need to tell you that child abuse has become the flavour of the moment, women as a whole carry a good deal more clout than they used to and they are now prepared to stand up and be counted, too much so at times with the false memory syndrome encouraged by some psychiatrists and counsellors.'

'And what's your reaction to that, Sinclair?'

'I have been thinking on exactly the same lines and I'm convinced that Fiona is right, but the problem is that we have no solid evidence against Hammond and what's more, Watson's taken both of us off the case until after the inquest, although permanently would be a great deal more likely in view of the words he used to me and his body language.'

Rawlings gave one of his sinister smiles. 'And so any more digging would be very difficult if not impossible for you, would it not, with Hammond's fellow board member and tame lap dog, Hastings, keeping a tight rein on you through Watson? I wish you luck, although I suspect you'll need a good deal more than that, and if I can help in any way, just let me know and that applies to both of you.'

11

Sinclair reckoned he could almost have written the script of the two inquests, which both he and Fiona attended. At the first one, after Margaret Rainsford had described how she had found Sophie and Bert Harris had given a detailed account of what he had discovered in her room, Rawlings was called to give the evidence he had found at the post-mortem. He did stick to his conclusion that she had not died as the result of alcohol and the drugs, evidence of which he had found in her blood, but not in concentrations that would have been likely to kill her, and that she had suffocated. He went on to say that he had found no evidence of injury, but that she had undoubtedly been sexually experienced. To Sinclair's relief, his approach was low key and he stuck strictly to the facts, not even mentioning the possibility of her having been murdered. At least, he thought, that might result in Hammond believing that he had got away with it and might lead to him lowering his guard while further enquiries were made about him.

Margaret Rainsford was then called back

and told the court that the girl had been very quiet and withdrawn, with no real friends, but had seemed to be settling in and was taking advantage of the excellent facilities for swimming and the coaching she was receiving and that she was coping well with her school work.

'I suspect you have already divined the way in which I have been thinking, Dr Rawlings,' the coroner said. 'Death was clearly secondary to respiratory failure and the influence of alcohol and the drugs you described. The question remains as to whether these were taken deliberately with suicidal intent or not. The evidence clearly points to this girl having been deeply disturbed and to have been behaving in a way that is unfortunately only too common these days. I have to take into account that there was no suicide note, but she was clearly an unhappy person, being friendless and withdrawn and had clearly been sucked into the drug culture.

'I dislike open verdicts, but I see no alternative to bringing that in. Let me say in unequivocal terms that no possible blame can be laid on the shoulders of her parents, or the college and my sympathies go to all those who tried to help this sadly troubled girl.'

As to Jo Roberts, the verdict was accidental death. In the coroner's view the cut on her head and the blood stains on the edge of the springboard made it clear that she had misjudged her jump with tragic consequences. Perhaps it had been rash of her to be carrying out complicated dives when on her own, but she was obviously an experienced and able diver and gymnast and had no doubt done such dives hundreds of times without mishap.

Sinclair badly needed a break and time for reflection and managed to arrange a couple of week's golf in Scotland with a friend from his days at Oxford. The fresh air, keen competition and good food did wonders for him. He was able to forget the frustrations of his job, the unsatisfactory outcome of the Sophie Hammond case and even his future, deliberately putting them out of his mind. He couldn't put them off any longer, though, when he got back and before returning to work went to see Bob Appleyard in London.

'I just can't go on working with that old woman, Watson, nor that idiot of a Chief Constable, Hastings,' he said, when he had told him that he was convinced that Clive Hammond was not only a child abuser, but had masterminded the murder of his adopted daughter and the woman who had carried it out. 'For good measure, too he is almost certainly involved in drugs, prostitution and burglary. The most depressing thing is that I can't see what can be done about it. I did have one idea which was to persuade the team that are working on the files on that paedophile website in America, which the FBI passed across to them, to see if by any chance Hammond's credit card details were on it.'

'And were they?'

'No such luck. I reckon that if he did access the site, he's far too wily a bird not to have used an untraceable account. The expert I spoke to admitted that their trawl is most likely to pick up the curious and minor players, rather than those seriously involved in the trade.

'I didn't get anywhere with that flat in Earls Court, either. The sergeant from the Yard told me the day after our visit there that the birds had flown when she went to check again and the landlord had no idea who was renting it — the money had been paid to the managing agent in cash by recorded delivery on a regular basis. Not surprisingly, the agent denied any knowledge of the purpose for which it was being used and I don't think that that line's going to get me anywhere, either.'

'What about those country house burglaries and the killing of the elderly woman you were telling me about?'

'That has been just as frustrating. After the inquests, Watson told me that the team who had been investigating it took the line that Jo Roberts must have been solely responsible for the whole business and that the case was closed. He tried to soft soap me by congratulating me on finding the DNA evidence before her accident and when I told him that she couldn't possibly have done it all on her own, in particular the disposal of the proceeds and that the organisation or organisations behind her at the health club and stunt school ought to be investigated, he said that the Chief Constable in question had decided that resources couldn't be wasted on such idle speculation. He as good as told me not to rock the boat, although, of course, he wasn't as direct as that.'

'I see your problems and how about that assistant of yours, who was clearly getting on your nerves, too?'

'Well, at least that one's been solved. Rawlings, who is our forensic pathologist, and who with our scene-of-crime man, Harris, are just about the only members of our team for whom I have respect, has taken her on as a lab technician. He has just got funding and is hoping to train her up to becoming a scientist in that field. I'm very happy for her; she's very able, but hasn't the right temperament for working in the front line of criminal investigation — she identifies too readily with victims. I believe, though, that she'll make a real success of working at one remove from that world.'

'And as to yourself?'

'I've thought long and hard about that and it's either a transfer, or getting out altogether.'

'We could certainly do with you up here. Early retirement for medical reasons has become a major scandal in my view and we're bleeding faster than a haemophiliac and badly need help. From what you've said, too, a case might well be made for some serious enquiries being instituted into the business and other activities of your friend, Clive Hammond.'

★   ★   ★

'I have decided to come to the inquest with you, Clive.'

'Do you think that's wise, dear? You know how upset you've been and all the distressing details will only make it worse.'

'I realise that, but if I'm going to get over this, I just have to know exactly how and why Sophie came to die.'

'Forgive me, you're right and, as you say, we have to help each other over this. I realise, of course, that you think I'm unemotional, too much so in fact, and again you're right, but you mustn't believe for one moment that I haven't been deeply upset by the whole business, too.'

Celia gave him a hug and with his answering smile, she felt closer to him than she had done for a very long time and knew, just knew, that everything was going to be all right between them.

He drove her to the court in the Mercedes and once there, held her hand and did so throughout the proceedings, periodically giving it a gentle squeeze. Celia listened to all the evidence, shaking her head from time to time and dabbing her eyes at intervals. The dry litany of drugs, alcohol, contraceptives and sexual activity, recounted directly and without emotion was almost more than she could bear. How had the sweet little girl, who was always so cheerful, have descended into the morose, rude and secretive child and adolescent she had become? Had she herself been responsible in some way for it? The coroner having gone to some lengths to say that neither she nor Clive were in any way to blame was some consolation, but hardly made it much better.

As they left the court, Celia momentarily caught sight of the pale detective constable, who had been so nice to her when she had come to the house. The young woman had her eyes fixed on Clive, her mouth was in a tight line, her forehead furrowed and she shook her head ever so slightly, but then the tall detective by her side whispered something in her ear and she suddenly relaxed, even managing an almost imperceptible nod and smile in Celia's direction and the moment was over.

Clive didn't say anything until they were on the main road and the car picked up speed.

'I don't quite know how to put this, Celia, but we've got to tackle it sooner or later. I had some friends before we were married and they lost a seventeen-year-old son with leukaemia and they made a shrine out of his bedroom. They showed it to me when I went round there for dinner and I thought it was one of the saddest things I'd ever seen — all his personal things were there, his posters, his sports' kit and so on and it was only too obvious that they'd not been able to move on, even though it had happened ten years earlier. I desperately don't want the same thing to happen to us and I think we should dispose of Sophie's clothes and any personal items in her room; after all, you've got all those lovely photo albums as mementos. Of course there's no desperate hurry, but you do see the point, don't you, and I'm sure Maria would help you?'

Celia didn't reply, staring straight through the windscreen, the tears coursing down her cheeks.

'Maybe this isn't the right time to have brought it up, but when is the right time after an appalling tragedy like this has hit us. You know better than anyone else that I'm not the sort of person to show emotions, but believe me, I'm not made of stone and I just knew that the longer I left it, the more difficult it would become for both of us.'

They were almost back home before Celia managed to get control of herself.

'You're right, of course, Clive,' she said. 'I keep thinking that in some way I must have been responsible for what happened, but I did try to do my best to communicate with Sophie and find out what was wrong and I know just how hard you did, too.'

When they had driven into the garage, he leaned across and held her tightly for a few moments.

'I don't believe it was anyone's fault, least of all yours; you could not have been a better mother to Sophie. We will just have to accept that some people are born with an addictive personality; it's not their fault, either, and once they get hooked, particularly on drugs such as cocaine and heroin, they are no longer themselves and they will do anything, absolutely anything to feed that addiction.'

As so often before, Celia felt herself buried under the force of her husband's personality; it wasn't that he ever lost his temper with her — he never did that — he just ground her down with his remorseless and unemotional logic. He had brought some work with him to do at home and while he locked himself in his study, she went for a long walk. The trouble was, she thought, that in many ways what Clive had said was true; it was futile to blame herself, or him, for that matter, for what had happened to Sophie, as they both, in their different ways had tried as hard as they could to get closer to her.

That evening, after they had watched one of the nature programmes that she so enjoyed, she was having a relaxing bath, when Clive came in, something she had never known him do before.

'Don't be too long, will you, my dear?' he said, looking at her with an intensity that sent a cold shiver right through her.

It was the first time he had come to her since they had heard the news about Sophie and it was like nothing she had experienced with him before. He did things to her that she had read about, but never experienced before and although some of it hurt, he drove her wild with excitement. By the end she was left utterly exhausted, but at the same time at peace for the first time in months. He didn't spoil it, either, by leaving her when it was all over, staying until she was fast asleep and the following morning, it was he rather than Maria who brought her breakfast up to her room.

After the housekeeper had helped her to remove all Sophie's belongings and agreed to take the clothes and her collection of tapes and CD's to a charity shop, Celia did a last check. It was at the back of the cupboard on top of the built-in wardrobe that she found Sophie's battered old teddy bear. All the time she had been helping Maria, Celia had managed to maintain tight control over herself, but that was the last straw. She took the bear through into her room, threw herself on to the bed and let go completely, holding it tightly to her chest and sobbing her heart out.

She was lying there, utterly spent, still clutching the bear, when all of a sudden, she sat bolt upright. She knew that bear, Oscar, well. A puppy they had had for a time several years earlier had had a free-for-all with it and had made a serious rent in its back. Sophie, who was eight at the time had been very upset and Celia had made a big production of the repair of the tear. While the small girl gave the anaesthetic, she had acted as surgeon, replacing some of the stuffing that had come out with cotton wool, trimming the edges and then sewing it up. It had been a time when Sophie was particularly withdrawn and to Celia's relief she had actually smiled and given her a hug when Oscar had been bandaged and put to bed. On a number of occasions subsequently she had had to repair the stitching, which had come loose, and she knew exactly what its back looked like and how it felt.

Now, it was quite different; there was a definite firm resistance when she squeezed it that had not been there before and when she inspected the stitching, she knew that it wasn't hers — it was just too even, neat and precise. Very carefully, she cut it with her nail scissors and put her fingers inside. Even before she had taken it out, she knew what it was, but where was the recorder to go with the mini cassette? Sophie had had one of that size, but it had been taken away by the police and not returned, presumably due to someone's oversight. As for Clive, she had no idea if he had one in his study. It was always kept locked and no one was allowed in there, not her, nor Maria — he even did his own cleaning when it was required — and whenever he was not in there, the heavy curtains were always drawn as well.

She suddenly remembered what Sophie had said just before she went to Sandford College: 'You'll look after my things while I'm away, won't you, mum, particularly Oscar? I know the other girls would laugh at me if I took him with me, so I'm relying on you.' Why oh why hadn't she realised what an odd request that was considering that Sophie had hardly said a word to her for weeks and that on that occasion there had been tears in her eyes?

Celia took down her case with the combination lock on it from the cupboard above her wardrobe and after putting both the bear and the cassette inside, she replaced it and went for a long walk through the wood nearby.

By the time she had got back, she knew what she was going to do if her suspicions proved to be correct, but first she had to listen to what was on the cassette and buying another recorder would be far too risky — if Clive either saw it or found out that she had bought one, he would certainly want to know the reason why. She was determined to think about every step she took as carefully as possible — after all, there was no hurry and before she went for her next hair appointment, she looked through the Yellow Pages and made several calls from the pay phone near the station. After that, it was just a question of finding a credible reason for going up to London.

The opportunity arose when she went to the coffee morning and demonstration of flower arranging that Rachel Kershaw had organised for one of her favourite charities. Celia liked Rachel; she was a direct no-nonsense sort of person, who was the only one of her friends not to be embarrassed about ringing up directly she had heard about Sophie and she had done so again to invite her to the event, telling her that not only would she be more than welcome, but that it would be good for her.

'I don't know why it is that people like you who have had to face a terrible tragedy are virtually ostracised,' she said, 'but for whatever reason there is, I'm not going to let it happen to you. You will come, won't you?'

As it turned out, Celia did enjoy it and the woman followed it up just as she was leaving.

'I've got a couple of tickets for a talk on Victorian dresses at the V and A next Wednesday; it should be good, a lot of them are going to be demonstrated by models. Care to come?'

Celia didn't hesitate. 'I'd love to. I can't thank you enough, I . . . '

She broke off, feeling the tears gathering.

'Think nothing of it; you'll be doing me a favour. That dreadful old gossip, Joan Armitage, knows that I won the tickets at a raffle and was angling for an invitation. What a relief it is that you can come! How about lunch at the restaurant beforehand? Meet you there at 12.30. All right?'

Celia did her very best to concentrate on what Rachel was saying at lunch and at the show and to make appropriate comments herself; it wouldn't have been easy anyway, but it was even less so when the mini cassette and the full size one, on to which she had been able to copy the contents, were resting in her handbag. It had been much simpler than she had feared; the man at the shop which had advertised the transfer of old film to video and from one audio tape to another, had set up the machines for her and then left her to press the appropriate buttons.

She couldn't face listening to the contents of the tape there and then and even left it until the following day, knowing that she wouldn't be able to face Clive at supper if half of what she suspected turned out to be true. As it was, she found herself telling him all about the talk and exhibition with such animation that he began to look at her, a quizzical expression on his face.

'I'm so glad you enjoyed it,' he said. 'You ought to do more things like that.'

His smile was so warm that she almost felt guilty about her suspicions, but all that changed when she drove into a parking place in the woods near Stoke d'Abernon and slotted the new cassette into the machine in her car.

Throughout, Sophie spoke in her soft, rather little-girl voice, monotonously and without expression or emotion, which some-how made the whole thing all the more distressing and poignant. It had begun when she was only six. Her mother had been so pleased when Clive wanted to be involved with his sweet little step-daughter right from the beginning of their marriage, but games with soap in the bath led to this and that, there were embraces when he kissed her goodnight and so it went on. A visit to the zoo on her own with him — he told Celia that that would be such a good way of getting to know her better — was followed a few weeks later by tea at the big house of one his friends in Regent's Park and it was there that she danced for them. What could be more natural than that she should try out some of the lovely costumes the man had in the big trunk and that they should have taken a video film of her performing? She hadn't noticed that the camera was running when she was changing and that when her stepfather was helping her she just happened to have nothing on at all for several minutes.

That was only the very beginning. There were other tea parties, mock punishments when she was made to recount the instances of minor acts of naughtiness at home after which she would receive a real, but very gentle spanking, on her bare bottom, of course. It had seemed quite fun at first, but then, very gradually, the blows became harder, there was a strap and then a cane, all of which were filmed. 'You're quite the little actress, aren't you?' one of the men had said and she was rewarded with chocolate cake and the type of ice cream she liked best.

Although she could hardly bear to do so, Celia listened to the rest of the tape with mounting distress and anger. Everything perverted that she had ever heard of and other acts that she hadn't, were gradually introduced and repeated over the years that followed. Why, she asked herself during the appalling catalogue, had Sophie not told her or someone in authority about it? After all, for several years there had been enough publicity about help lines. That was soon answered;

they had shown her photographs of people who had crossed or threatened to inform on them and the worst of them was that of the girl who had been permanently disfigured by acid thrown into her face, an image that remained imprinted on her mind and was the cause of vivid and terrifying nightmares.

It was when she reached adolescence that Clive and his fellow paedophiles lost interest in her and he told her that he didn't want her creeping around the house the whole time and that he had decided to send her away to boarding school. On the tape, Sophie made it clear that she was still worried about what her stepfather might be planning for her, but at least she would be safe at school and have time to decide what she was going to do.

★   ★   ★

Celia sat staring through the windscreen for a long time after the cassette was over. She went through all the whys — why hadn't she realised what was going on, why hadn't Sophie said anything about it at all, why had she herself been so easily taken in by Clive — and found many of the answers. She had been very depressed herself by what she believed to be Sophie's drug taking and had no one to turn to and it was perfectly clear that Sophie believed Clive's threats, as Celia knew she would have done herself and lastly, he could be very subtle and persuasive. Why else had she married him, believing it would be the answer to all her problems, when it was only too obvious now that he had done so only to get Sophie into his clutches? He had been so understanding about her own past difficulties and she had even believed that his lack of interest in her sexually was because he thought she had suffered enough in that direction. The final insult had been what he had done to her that night after the inquest, when he was obviously on a high, believing that with Sophie out of the way and no blame having been attached to him at the inquest, he had got away with it.

After all the immediate distress and recriminations, what was left was steely determination. She was going to kill Clive, kill him for Sophie's sake, her own sake and the sake of other children who had suffered or were going to suffer at his hands unless she did something about it. The police would be useless and in any case, she doubted very much if the evidence of the tape, which was all she had, would be enough to get him convicted and she was also honest enough to admit that, more importantly, she was terrified of what might happen to her if he or his associates ever found out that she had been responsible for handing it over.

There was something else that suddenly hit her with a force that was almost physical. Clive had murdered Sophie; how he had done it hardly mattered, she just had no doubt about it in her mind at all. She suddenly remembered the expression on the police-woman's face at the inquest. The young woman obviously believed that Clive had been responsible for Sophie's death and if she and the other detective weren't able to pin it on him, then what chance had she?

Celia had no immediate idea about how to set about it, but she would find a way and if she could do it covertly, so well and good, but if it meant sacrificing herself, so be it.

★ ★ ★

To Celia's amazement, in the weeks that followed she felt more alive than she had done for years. She spent hours on the internet and in the public library in Kingston and even longer than that just thinking. Clive even noticed the change in her, too; she saw him looking at her one evening at supper in a way that left her anxious and unable to get to sleep after she had gone to bed, terrified that he might come to her again. What made it worse was that she knew that she couldn't afford to refuse him if he did. He had always been able to read her like a book and perhaps he already suspected that she was up to something.

The idea came to her very gradually and the first thing she decided on was the method. Any form of violence was out of the question; she just hadn't that sort of personality and knew that if it came to it, she wouldn't be able to carry it through. As to engineering an accident, say with his car, that wouldn't be certain enough and anyway she hadn't got the necessary expertise and had no intention of involving anyone else. And so, she decided that it would have to be done with drugs and there would be the added bonus of knowing that if she was successful it would be poetic justice for what had happened in Sophie's case.

The proceedings at the inquest were etched on her memory and she remembered the drug rohypnol being mentioned, already being aware of the publicity over it in its connection with 'date rape'. She soon discovered on the internet and the pharmacopoeia that she found in the library in Kingston that it was one of the group of sedative and anxiety relieving drugs called benzodiazepines and that they were commonly used for sleeping difficulties.

Overdose seldom seemed to be fatal, but that wasn't part of the plan she had been thinking about.

The next problem was getting hold of one of that group of drugs. Obviously, they would only be available on prescription and one possibility might be going to a private GP in Harley Street and giving a false name. She wasn't all that happy with the idea and soon found a method that was much easier and less risky.

With the improvement in her mood and growing friendship with Rachel Kershaw, she had begun to invite people to coffee and lunch at the house when Clive was at work and was soon asked back. That gave her the opportunity to look through people's medicine cabinets when she used their bathrooms and it was in one of them that she discovered the plastic container, almost full of white tablets. The label on it had the name mogadon printed on it, with instructions on how to take it and underneath, in small print, nitrazepam, BP. Realising that such a good opportunity might not arise again, she took out about twenty of them, wrapped them in a tissue and slipped them into her handbag. There was an empty small clear-glass bottle in her bathroom and, using a pair of the very fine disposable gloves that she used from time to time to clean her jewellery, she wiped it carefully with her hand towel to get rid of any fingerprints and put the tablets into it. The following day, she looked up the drug on the internet, found that it belonged to the same chemical group as rohypnol, was also quick acting and when she crushed one up and tasted it, found that it was rather bitter. Much more difficult than that problem, though, was working out the best way to get Clive to take it, but in the end she found one that seemed promising. She went over and over it in her mind and knew that with average luck it should not only work, but she stood a good chance of getting away with it, not that that was in the forefront of her mind.

Clive was a creature of habit and every Sunday morning, when he was at home, he liked to stretch out on the lounger by the pool, wearing his trunks and a towelling robe, and read the Sunday newspapers, of which he took several. More often than not, he would go for a swim afterwards, but before that, precisely at ten-thirty, she would bring him a mug of cappuccino and one chocolate biscuit and then leave him in peace. It was the one thing he liked her to do for him, because the Petaccis always went to Mass at that time and although she felt reasonably confident that the liberal topping of chocolate powder and sugar that he liked would hide both the sight of the ground up tablets and their grittiness and the bitterness, she decided to put it properly to the test. She prepared a mug of the coffee in exactly the same way as she always did for Clive and then added one crushed-up tablet after another, tasting the mixture carefully after vigorous stirring each time, until the bitterness became obvious. Five of the pills were, she decided, the maximum possible. From time to time, too, the Italian couple went down to Hove on a Sunday to have lunch with Luigi's brother who ran a restaurant down there and that would be the time to do it.

It was a Sunday in May when everything came together. The Petaccis were planning to leave after the breakfast had been cleared and Celia had rung Rachel Kershaw earlier in the week, who had agreed with evident pleasure to accept her invitation to have lunch at Wisley gardens and afterwards to look at the azaleas and rhododendrons. That only left the rest of her alibi to be worked out.

After a great deal of thought, she came up with the solution, which was to use Clive's old watch. It was the one he had always taken on holidays — he had an absolute obsession with time and wouldn't be without one, even on the beach and wasn't going to risk his gold

Rolex in that situation, either, locking it up in the safe in his study whenever they went away. She didn't know where he kept the other one, but eventually found it in one of the small drawers in the built-in wardrobe in his bedroom. She remembered teasing him about the fact that a man, who prided himself in always having the latest gadgets, should use a watch that needed to be wound up, but as always, to her irritation, he both had a good reason for choosing it and the last word. 'It's not only for holidays, you know,' he had said, 'I always wear it when I'm helping Luigi in the garden and what use is a battery or solar operated one in a situation like that?' It was true, he did help the Italian outside when he felt in the need of some exercise in the fresh air and as a variation on his usual run on the treadmill, which was in a recess at the end of the pool.

Using another pair of the gloves, Celia partially wound up the watch, checked that it was working, then half-filled the basin in her bedroom and dropped it in. When she came back an hour later, she found to her relief and satisfaction that it had stopped. She dried the outside carefully, put it back where she had found it and after that, it was just a question of waiting.

The Sunday dawned fine, the Italians drove

off at ten and once she had checked that Clive was on the lounger by the pool with the Sunday paper, she went into the kitchen. She could have prepared the cappuccino with her eyes shut, but she did it with the greatest care, grinding up five of the remaining mogadon tablets until the resulting powder was as fine as she was able to get it. A final vigorous stir after she had added rather more sugar than normal was followed by the sprinkling of a liberal amount of the chocolate topping on the frothy coffee and then, as she always did at precisely ten-thirty, took it through to him.

'Thank you, my dear, right on time as usual,' Clive said with a smile as she put it down on the low table by his side.

Clive's routine on a Sunday morning was sacrosanct and never varied. He liked to be left alone by the pool and she never chatted to him at that time and on this occasion, desperate though she was to make sure that he had drunk the coffee, she behaved exactly the same way as she always did, leaving him an answering smile.

'Maria has left your lunch under cling-film on the kitchen table and there is some beer in the fridge if you feel like it,' she said.

He gave her an answering nod and without saying another word, she went back through the glass doors into the living-room.

She was due to pick Rachel up in her car at noon and she waited until just before eleven-thirty, when she walked briskly back to the poolside, determined not to creep in there in case Clive had not taken the drink, or else the drug had not worked. He was still stretched out on the lounger and as she approached she saw that the mug was empty and that the spoon was inside it.

'Clive,' she said and then louder. 'Clive!'

There was no response, he was breathing heavily and she went upstairs to collect his watch, once again wearing the thin gloves. After that, she went down to the kitchen and picked up the battery operated cassette recorder, which she had bought with cash in a large London store a couple of weeks earlier, together with the tape inside it, the empty bottle which had contained the mogadon tablets — she had flushed all the remaining ones down the lavatory — and a glass containing a small amount of water. Back at the pool, she put all the items she was carrying down on the table and when she was absolutely satisfied that her husband was still deeply unconscious, still wearing the gloves, she took off his watch, substituted his old one which she had set to one forty-two, and then put his right hand round the glass, lifting it

278

up and pressing it against his lips before returning it to the table. Having made sure that his fingerprints were also on the empty tablet bottle, she pressed his hands on to the tape recorder in various places and then pushed his forefinger hard down on the start button. She could not bear to hear Sophie's voice again, so once she was satisfied that the volume control was set at the right level, she switched it off.

There was a pair of wheels at the head of the lounger and by lifting up the foot it was a simple matter to manoeuvre it so that it was parallel to the edge of the pool. She changed her position so that she was standing half way along it, then gripped the edge with both hands, bent her knees and started to straighten her back. For several anxious moments after she had managed to lift it about six inches, she thought she wasn't going to be able to do it, but then Clive began to roll sideways and with a loud splash hit the water. To her horror, he floated face downwards and she had to fetch a broom from the kitchen and press down on his back with it. A series of bubbles came up from the air trapped in his robe and very slowly he sank to the bottom.

It took her a good fifteen minutes to put the lounger back to where it had been, wash up the coffee mug in the kitchen, take the gold watch she had removed from Clive's wrist up to his bedroom and change for her visit to Wisley. When she came down again, her husband was still lying on the floor of the pool, mercifully head down, and everything seemed to be in order until she suddenly remembered that she had failed to switch the recorder on again and, using her handkerchief to protect it from her finger, she pressed the start button, adjusted the volume and then left hurriedly to the sound of Sophie's flat voice, which would haunt her for the rest of her days.

Celia had been playing a part with Clive ever since she had heard the tape for the first time, but she was always to remember that afternoon at Wisley with Rachel as the best performance of her life. Her new friend was never short of things to say, which made it easier, but Celia kept her end up, chatting away more easily than she usually did, she ate a good lunch and afterwards they walked round for at least two hours, enjoying the magnificent display of azaleas and rhododen-drons.

'Why not come back to our place for a cup of tea?' Rachel said as they made their way back to the car park.

'Thank you, I'd love to. Clive's bound to be

beavering away at something or other — as usual.'

'I don't know how you put up with him — talk about workaholic.'

Celia drove carefully through the gates of her house just before 6.30. There was a police car in the drive and as she went in through the front door, she heard sobbing coming from the kitchen. The young policewoman in uniform was trying to comfort the hysterical Maria and she straightened up as she heard Celia open the door.

'Mrs Hammond?'

'Yes.'

'I'm afraid I have very bad news for you.'

12

Mark Sinclair had just finished breakfast and was listening to the radio in the kitchen while he did the small amount of washing up, when he heard the paper being pushed through the letter box. He went into the hall of his flat and had just picked it up when the phone rang only three feet away from him.

'Sinclair here.'

'Still in bed are you, you lazy devil?'

The detective grinned, recognising Rawlings's rasping tones straight away.

'*Au contraire*, I'm just off to work. I don't recommend this commuting business, though and I'm going to have to move.'

'Don't blame you. Read the paper yet?'

'No, it's only come this minute.'

'Try page four. I'll make some enquiries and perhaps you'd give me a ring after nine, this evening.'

It was no mystery to Sinclair that Rawlings should have known that they both took the same paper — they had often practised a bit of one-upmanship over clues in the crossword — and he found the paragraph straight away.

DEATH IN SWIMMING POOL

Successful entrepreneur and millionaire, Clive Hammond, was found drowned in the swimming pool at his luxury home near Esher last Sunday afternoon. His wife, who was visiting a friend at the time, told our reporter that her husband had been depressed since the tragic death of their sixteen year old only daughter, who took her own life some months ago.

For once, Sinclair didn't start the crossword on the train. He was quite certain that Hammond hadn't committed suicide, it would have been totally out of character, and having watched him like a hawk at Sophie's inquest, there had not been the slightest hint of strain or distress on his face. He said as much to Rawlings on the phone that evening.

'Well,' the pathologist replied, 'you've had the advantage of meeting him, but from what I've heard, I got the same impression. I'm afraid I haven't got anywhere so far — the Surrey people are in charge of the case — but I'll see what I can do in the next day or two. Why not come to lunch on Sunday and I'll see if I can get Fiona Campbell along, too?'

* ★ ★

'Well, what have I got up my sleeve?' Rawlings said when they were sitting in the drawing-room with their coffee after lunch. 'More than you might think. You see, Brandon, the man who did the autopsy, is an old protégé of mine and he's come up with some interesting information.' The pathologist reached down and opened the folder on the floor beside him. 'I haven't been able to get all the details, but Hammond was found by the Italian couple, who act as gardener and housekeeper, on the floor of the pool at his house.' He handed across a photograph. 'They made no attempt to get him out — the woman evidently threw a major wobbly, as our Australian friends are in the habit of saying, and the man had his hands full with her and just dialled 999. As you see from this photograph, Hammond was lying face down on the bottom of the pool and was wearing swimming trunks and a towelling robe. His watch had stopped at 1.42 and a considerable, but non-lethal, level of nitrazepam was found in his blood. Death was due to drowning and there was no other abnormality and, in particular, no injuries.

'His wife evidently went to Wisley that day with a woman friend, who is the wife of a solicitor, with a practice in Kingston. She picked the woman up soon after midday, they drove straight to the botanical gardens, had lunch, then spent the whole afternoon walking round and finished up with a cup of tea back at the woman's house. She stayed there until just after six and then returned home. The woman friend was evidently interviewed and confirmed it all.

'This photograph is also of interest, showing the table by the side of the lounger. The glass had the man's fingerprints on it and the DNA found on the rim where he had taken a drink was his. Likewise, his prints were on the bottle, which had contained the nitrazepam — there was still some powder left in it.'

'That's odd,' said Sinclair. 'I can't believe that in what seems an open and shut case like this, they would normally have gone to that degree of trouble and what about the tape recorder that I can see there?'

'As usual, you've hit the nail on the head, my dear fellow, why indeed? I've tried to find out what was on the cassette in the recorder and all Brandon would say was that it contained nothing of any great interest. Now, I reckon I'm as good as the next man in telling when someone is lying and he was — I have no doubt of it. Now why?'

'Any views, Fiona?' Sinclair asked.

'If Hammond didn't commit suicide and I agree he didn't seem to be the type, then either it was an accident, which seems an absurd suggestion, or else he was murdered. In any event, the cassette may provide the answer and if it just contained say recorded music, why didn't the pathologist say so?'

'I couldn't have put it better myself,' Rawlings said. 'I'm most certainly going to attend the inquest and no doubt both of you will want to as well.'

★   ★   ★

At the inquest into Sophie's death, Sinclair had only had eyes for the Hammonds; both of them had been very much in control of themselves and it had been early in the proceedings that he had seen the man take hold of his wife's hand, which he continued to do throughout. Now, he watched Celia Hammond equally carefully. On this occasion she was with another woman, who from time to time whispered something into her ear.

The medical evidence was exactly as Rawlings had described earlier. The Italian woman, who spoke much better English than her husband and although tearful from time to time, was able to give her evidence clearly enough. She told the court that the two of them had left the house that Sunday at the same time, 10.00 a.m., as they always did when going down to Hove for their lunch date. Yes, Mr Hammond had seemed his usual self that morning and had followed his normal routine on a Sunday morning. No, they had not made any attempt to get him out; she was ashamed of the way she had reacted, but, in any case, neither of them were able to swim, he was on the bottom of the pool at the deep end and, in any case, he would have been too heavy for them to lift.

The coroner was gentle with her and assured her that neither of them could be criticised for what they had done and then it was Celia Hammond's turn. Obviously nervous throughout her evidence, twisting her handkerchief with her fingers, she explained that she had made her husband's coffee, as she always did on a Sunday morning, and then departed as he liked to be left alone while he read the Sunday paper and she had gone back at about eleven forty just before leaving for her lunch date both to say goodbye and to tell him that Maria had left his lunch under cling-film on the kitchen table. Questioned about the coffee, she said that she had made it herself, which she always did, and took the mug back to the kitchen and washed it up before leaving to pick up her friend. She confirmed that he had seemed his usual self earlier that morning and when she left him. No, she hadn't seen the bottle of pills — perhaps he had gone up to his room to fetch it after she had left, or else it might have been in the pocket of his robe. When asked if her husband was in the habit of taking sleeping tablets, she replied that she didn't know as they did not share a bedroom — he liked to go to bed late and was always up by 6.00 a.m. He had suggested the arrangement right from the start of their marriage as he didn't want to disturb her. It was true, she said that her husband was not a man to show his emotions, but he had undoubtedly been very affected by Sophie's death. Like her, he wondered if he could have done more to protect their daughter from herself and the move to Sandford College had been something they had discussed and it had seemed to be the only way forward. No, he never talked about business affairs with her. Finally she was asked about the tape recorder found on the table by the pool. She was quite sure it hadn't been there when she brought him his coffee, nor when she took the mug away to wash it up, indeed there had been nothing else on the table at all. As to the recorder itself, she had never seen it before.

There was a double one as part of their sound system in the drawing-room and she had one in her car, but the only other one in the house, as far as she knew, had been in Sophie's room and that had been taken away by the police. Her husband had then asked them to dispose of it when they had finished with it.

Finally, one of the investigating officers gave evidence about Hammond's watch, which was found to contain water and which had stopped at 1.42 and he also stated that the man had not touched the lunch that had been left for him in the kitchen.

'You've heard the medical evidence that death was due to drowning and that nitrazepam, which clearly had come from the bottle on the table, was found in a high concentration in the deceased's blood. Although this was insufficient to have proved fatal it would have rendered him unconscious. His watch had stopped at 1.42 at a time when we know that he had been alone in the house for roughly two hours. Why, as it would appear, did the deceased take both sleeping tablets and then drown himself, rather than do one or the other? Perhaps he knew that there weren't enough tablets in the bottle to prove fatal and when he began to feel drowsy, entered the water and sank down as he became unconscious. Clearly, it will never be known exactly what was going on in his mind and we have heard how he always kept tight control of his emotions. The tragic death of his daughter must have proved too much for him and I find therefore, that he took his own life while the balance of his mind was disturbed.'

Rawlings joined Sinclair and Fiona in the car park.

'Still no mention of the tape recorder,' I note, said the pathologist.

'Exactly, but I heard on the grapevine that the people in London who are buzzing around Hammond's business activities, are particularly interested in it and I have hopes of listening to it myself in the near future,' Sinclair replied.

★   ★   ★

It was six weeks later that Sinclair was at last given access to the tape, but he was not allowed to remove it from the building and Rawlings and Fiona had to come up to London to listen to it.

'I found it every bit as upsetting this time as the first time I heard it,' he said when it had run through, deliberately not looking in Fiona's direction as she wiped a tear away from her eye. 'The reason that the contents of the tape were not mentioned at the inquest was that the description you have just heard that Sophie gave of the house in Regent's Park and its proximity to the Royal College of Psychiatrists — pretty ironic that — together with other scraps of information the Vice Squad had got hold of, enabled it to be pin-pointed with reasonable accuracy. A watch was put on that particular terrace and the group of paedophiles was caught red-handed as another young girl was taken in, which is the one good thing that has come out of this sorry tale. As to the rest of Hammond's activities, robbery, money laundering, extortion, insider dealing, you name it, he did it. Prostitution was another of his big lines, involving mainly eastern Europe illegal immigrants, which is not exactly a surprise considering how he set up that scam in Earls Court to discredit Sophie.'

'I'm even more convinced than I was before that Hammond didn't commit suicide,' Fiona said.

Rawlings looked at her with a quizzical expression on his face. 'And why not, pray? Cause of death definitely drowning, a significant level of nitrazepam in the blood, a dusting of the drug in the bottle on the table by the lounger and not only his fingerprints on that, but on the glass, the cassette and tape recorder as well. For good measure his DNA was on the rim of the glass and his watch with some water in it had stopped at a time when no one else was in the house. To cap it all, both the man's wife and the Italian couple had cast iron alibis for that time.'

'It's all just a bit too neat and totally out of character, as I mentioned before. Anyway, without that tape we'd never have been able to pin Sophie's murder on him and why did it suddenly appear many months after her death?'

'He could have had it all along, listened to it from time to time and finally it might have got to him.'

'Yes, but can you see a man like him leaving it where it was bound to be found and thus landing his paedophile associates in such a vulnerable position?'

'Well, what do you think, Sinclair?'

'I agree with Fiona and apart from the logic behind that view, I have also only just found out an interesting extra piece of evidence that not only makes her suspicions very likely, but also points to the perpetrator.'

'Celia Hammond?' said Fiona.

'Why do you think that?' Rawlings asked.

'Because if I'd been Sophie's mother and then found the tape somewhere, that's what I might well have done myself.'

'Do you also think it was her, Sinclair?' Rawlings said. 'Come along, man, what's this magic bit of evidence you've got up your sleeve?'

'The watch. There was rust in it and the expert who looked at it said that he didn't think that it could have been functioning when Hammond went into the pool.'

'You mean that it was old rust?' Sinclair nodded. 'I see. So the woman was very clever, but not quite clever enough.'

'I wouldn't put it quite like that. You see, the crown prosecution service has looked at all the evidence and has decided that that of the watch on its own isn't strong enough to justify pursuing the matter any further.'

'And do you think that there's an element of 'Hammond's got what he deserved' in that decision?'

Sinclair lips twitched. 'Dr Rawlings, I'm shocked, what a suggestion!'

We do hope that you have enjoyed reading this large print book.

Did you know that all of our titles are available for purchase?

We publish a wide range of high quality large print books including:
Romances, Mysteries, Classics
General Fiction
Non Fiction and Westerns

Special interest titles available in large print are:
The Little Oxford Dictionary
Music Book
Song Book
Hymn Book
Service Book

Also available from us courtesy of Oxford University Press:
Young Readers' Dictionary
(large print edition)
Young Readers' Thesaurus
(large print edition)

For further information or a free brochure, please contact us at:
Ulverscroft Large Print Books Ltd.,
The Green, Bradgate Road, Anstey,
Leicester, LE7 7FU, England.
Tel: (00 44) 0116 236 4325
Fax: (00 44) 0116 234 0205

UNWILLINGLY TO SCHOOL

Peter Conway

Janet Creswell is struggling to come to terms with her husband's sudden death when she receives a visit from Richard Medley, a former pupil at Brantwood preparatory school in Sussex, where in 1944 she'd been matron. Their meeting evokes memories. However, it also raises serious doubts regarding the headmaster, Edward Blackstone, as well as questions about the maltreatment of the boys. And his drowning in the swimming pool — had it been an accident, or murder? Her curiosity piqued, Janet meets people involved in the school at that time, and finally discovers the truth about those distant, disturbing events.

LOCKED IN

Peter Conway

Is Father Carey a saint or sinner? Comforter of the sick — or a heavy drinker not to be trusted with secrets, confessional or otherwise? Opinion at St Cuthbert's Hospital is divided. Michael Donovan, paralysed after a rugby accident, views him as the only person to give him support. But when Father Carey is poisoned, Donovan loses the will to live. On a respirator and locked inside his paralysed body there is nothing he can do about it. Or is there? Though unable to speak or move, there is nothing inactive about his mind. Can he find a way to track down the killer?

WITH A NARROW BLADE

Faith Martin

When an elderly lady is stabbed to death in her own home, DI Hillary Greene is instantly puzzled. There's no appearance of a robbery; Flo Jenkins, popular with her neighbours, hadn't an enemy in the world. And everyone knew that, riddled with cancer, she'd only weeks left to live. Why kill a dying woman? Greene's investigation is not helped when her new DC turns out to have a violent temper and an uncertain past. With no forensics, no leads and only a junkie grandson as a suspect, is this going to be Hillary Greene's first failure on a murder case?

UNDER THE MANHATTAN BRIDGE

Irene Marcuse

After leaving her stressful job as a social worker Anita Servi is now helping her husband, Benno, in his woodworking shop and spending time in the arty community under the New York Manhattan Bridge. Then Anita discovers the hidden body of a young man who has been brutally murdered. There are no clues to his identity but plenty of questions needing answers. Finding the answer is something Anita knows how to do and she begins her search from the Lower East Side to the art galleries of the East Village. What she uncovers is revealed in a startling denouement . . .